CORROSION

Jon Bassoff

For Amanda,
a woman with soul.

Jon Bassoff

First Edition
ISBN 978-1-937771-80-5

A DarkFuse Release
www.darkfuse.com

Join the Newsletter:
http://eepurl.com/jOH5

Become a fan on Facebook:
www.facebook.com/darkfuse

Follow us on Twitter:
www.twitter.com/darkfuse

"Jon Bassoff's stream of conscious novel sports Faulkner-like as this dark tale is told in first person timelines. It will grip and engage and ultimately leave you shaken to the core. Not for the tenderhearted...not no way, not no how. *Corrosion* is the tale of a man on a mission from God...or is it the Devil? Dare to find out."

—Charlie Stella, author of *Johnny Porno*

"Talk about a book starting one way and then springing something on you...[Bassoff's *Corrosion*] is dark and funny and sick, a book as much about identity as it is about crime."

—Bill Crider, author of the Sheriff Dan Rhodes series

"*Corrosion* is a fever dream, a lucid nightmare. It is at once poetic and brutal; hypnotic and vicious; empathetic and heartless. It is the most effective kind of horror—the kind you believe. Reading it is a deeply uncomfortable experience in the best possible way."

—Marcus Sakey, author of *The Two Deaths of Daniel Hayes*

"An archetypal, nightmare journey down a hall of mirrors. *Corrosion* will burn your eyeballs. Keep you reading relentlessly to the end."

—Jonathan Woods, award-winning author of *Bad Juju & Other Tales of Madness and Mayhem* and *A Death in Mexico*.

Praise for Corrosion

"*Corrosion* is a beautifully bleak noir novel that stretches the boundaries of the genre to its breaking point. A virtuoso performance by the terrific Jon Bassoff."
— Jason Starr , International bestselling author of *The Craving*

"Like some unholy spawn of Cormac McCarthy's *Child of God* and Donald Ray Pollock's *The Devil All the Time*, *Corrosion* offers pungent writing, a cast of irresistibly damaged characters, and a narrative that's as twisted and audacious as any I have read in a long while. A dark gem."
— Roger Smith, author of *Dust Devils*

"Sharp, original, fierce, a real gut-ripper. *Corrosion* is one of the most startlingly original and unsettling novels I've read in ages. It ramps your pulse, it claws at your sweet spot. Bassoff has a career ahead of him brightly lit by a very bad star."
— Tom Piccirilli, author of Edgar Award-nominated novel *The Cold Spot*

"Imagine Chuck Palahniuk filtered through Tarantino speak, blended with an acidic Jim Thompson and a book that cries out to be filmed by David Lynch, then you have a flavor of *Corrosion*. The debut novel from the unique Jon Bassoff begins a whole new genre: Corrosive Noir."
— Ken Bruen, Shamus Award-winning author of *The Guards*

"Jon Bassoff gives new meaning to the phrase "Hell on earth" in his debut novel, *Corrosion*. It's a harrowing page-turning tale of lost, misplaced, and mangled identity that barrels its way to breakdowns and showdowns of literal and figurative biblical proportions."
— Lynn Kostoff, author of *Late Rain*

For my father.

Acknowledgement

Thanks to my incredible wife Tobey for putting up with a distracted and occasionally frustrated writer for more than a decade. Much thanks and love to the other strong and supportive women in my life, my mother, Evelyn, and my sister, Leah. Thanks also to my students and colleagues at Frederick High who have tolerated a more-than-slightly disturbed English teacher in their midst. I'm proud to call Allan Guthrie my agent and am forever indebted to him for his belief in my writing and his hard work in getting this thing published. And finally, I am grateful to Shane Staley, Greg F. Gifune, and the folks at DarkFuse for giving this book a home.

PART ONE:
JOSEPH DOWNS (2010)

"When I discover who I am, I'll be free."
—Ralph Ellison, *Invisible Man*

CHAPTER 1

I was less than 20 miles from the Mountain when the engine gave out, smoke billowed from the hood, and Red Sovine stopped singing. I pushed the old pickup for a while, but it was no use. She'd let me down good this time. I pulled her off to the side of the highway, kicked open the door, and cursed at the wind. I stared down the cracked highway; a backwater town was just up ahead, surrounded by derricks and grain elevators. I grabbed my army-issued duffel bag from the trunk, pulled on my camouflage jacket, and started limping down the asphalt.

The town was called Stratton, and it wasn't much. Just brick buildings and rotting bungalows and poor-man shacks all dropped haphazardly by God after a two-week bender. Old Main was hanging on for dear life. An abandoned convenience store, abandoned gas station, abandoned motel. Rusted signs and boarded-up windows.

The wind was blowing hard and mean; I pulled up the collar of my jacket and buried my hands in my pockets. I caught a glimpse of myself in a darkened window and shivered. It was a face that I still didn't recognize. A face that appeared to have been molded by the devil himself...

Twelve hours on the road and I was in bad need of a drink. At the corner of the block stood a white stucco building with the words *Del's Lounge* hand painted in red, a neon Bud sign glowing in a submarine window. I went inside.

The floor was concrete and the tables were wooden. There was a pool table with torn blue felt, and a jukebox, twenty years old at least. A burly fellow with a red handlebar mustache sat at the counter drinking from a Coors can, his overalls smeared with paint or blood, while an old man with a rosacea nose sat in a vinyl booth, arms cradling a tumbler of bourbon. The bartender — a skinny man with sickly yellow hair and liver spotted-hands — whistled a nameless tune and wiped down the counter lethargically. Head down, floor creaking, I walked across the room and sat at a corner table, back to the bar. I placed my bag on the floor and stuck a pinch of snuff between my gums and lower lip. After a few minutes, I heard footsteps. I didn't turn around. The bartender stood right behind me and asked me what I wanted, his voice all full of barbed wire.

Bottle of beer, I said. Cold.

Doncha want some food? We got hamburgers and hot dogs and the best barbecue pork in town.

All I wanted was the beer, but he moved so that he was in front of me and handed me a menu, and then he saw my face and said, Ah, Jesus. It was an involuntary reaction.

Just a beer, I said again.

He muttered an apology and walked back to the bar and everybody was looking—the same curious bystanders who watch in disguised glee every time there is a car wreck on the highway or a shooting outside a nightclub. I stared straight ahead, tapping the table with my fingers. The jukebox creaked into action and Merle Haggard started singing, but the speakers were busted and his voice was warbled, drunken.

The bartender came back a few minutes later with my beer. He could've left me alone, but he wanted to prove he wasn't frightened of me. He just stood there, jaw slack. He had a full set of bottom teeth, but nothing on the top. I could smell his breath, a strange combination of bourbon and candy canes. So, uh, what's your business here in Stratton? he said.

I cleared my throat. No business. How much do I owe you?

You don't owe me a penny. Drink's on the house.

I was used to it. I made a living off other people's pity. They'd bury me in a potter's field.

I took a long drink and wiped my mouth with my sleeve. I'm looking for a place to stay, I said. Someplace cheap.

The bartender smiled slyly. Everything is cheap in this town, he said, but the Hotel Paisano is cheaper than most. Just a few blocks down on Third.

Much obliged, I said.

I drank my beer, and then another and another, and then I heard a car pull up outside, the engine growling. The door slammed and I could hear a man and woman arguing outside, and the sound of a bottle shattering on asphalt. The man shouting Goddamn slut, you are!

A moment later, the door opened and a woman walked inside. She wasn't very pretty, but that sort of thing never mattered to me. She was tall and skinny with bright red hair swooped up in a sort of beehive. Her face was pale and her nose was crooked. She had a stud in her lip and a tattoo of Betty Page on her arm. She wore red boots and cut-off jeans and a Misfits T-shirt.

She stomped her way up to the bar and plopped down on a stool. Got Maker's Mark? she asked the bartender.

He wiped the sweat from his forehead and nodded. Yes, ma'am. How do you drink it?

Quickly, she said. And give me a Michelob, too.

The bartender pulled out a heavy-looking glass, poured a fistful of whiskey, and popped open a bottle of beer. She raised the glass and made a toast to all the bastards in the world before slugging it down. Then she coughed and grimaced and reached for the beer. I was hooked.

Not two moments later the man came charging in. He wore cowboy boots and tight blue jeans and a heavy flannel. His face was bloated and red, his mustache thick and gray. He was twice as old as the girl, easy.

He wanted her out of the bar and he said so, but she wasn't having any of it. Fuck you, she said. You're not my keeper.

This man strode to the counter with more than a

little purpose. He yanked the beer out of her hand and slammed it hard on the counter. The fellow with the bloodstained overalls rose to his feet and took a couple of cautious steps back. The bartender said, Now, just take it easy, mister. We don't want no trouble here. Me, I watched from a distance, seeing how it would all play out, because I wasn't a violent man except when I had to be...

Let's get out of here, you goddamn whore, the man said, and you could tell he meant business. She tried pulling away, and that's when he got rough with her. He grabbed a handful of her red hair and yanked her off the stool. The girl screamed. He let go of her hair but grabbed her arm, twisting it behind her back. She was flopping around like a rag doll.

I rose from my seat and walked unhurriedly across the bar. The old man didn't pay any attention to me, just kept twisting her arm tighter and tighter. I could feel the blood running in my veins.

Let go of her, I said, my voice barely louder than a whisper.

He looked up. Seeing my melted face distracted him, and he loosened his grip on the girl's arm. She managed to twist away for a moment, but he recovered and shoved her against the wall. I grabbed the bottle of beer from the counter, came up from behind, and slammed it on the back of his head. He wobbled around for a few moments before his legs gave way and he fell to the hardwood floor.

For a good long while he didn't do anything but moan and groan. Then he started moving, pulling himself across the floor, but there was no real conviction to his movements. Every time he tried getting

Corrosion

up I gave him a good hard kick to the stomach or the face. I wanted him to know a few things. His girl was pleading for me to stop but I knew she didn't mean it, that it was all for show. By the time I got through with him, he was curled up in a ball, coughing up blood, his face a pulpy mess.

I went back to my table, drank down the last swallow of my beer, and slung my bag over my shoulder. Everybody was watching me. I walked slowly toward the front of the bar, graveyard boots echoing on the cement. I stepped over the man and nodded at the bartender. The Paisano, right? I said.

Yes, sir. It ain't nothing fancy, but they'll treat you real good, yes they will.

I nodded my head at the girl and pushed open the door.

Wait! I heard her say. I turned around. She flashed a crooked grin, dark eyes filled with adulation. Who are you? What's your name?

My name's Joseph Downs, I said, and I served my country proudly.

CHAPTER 2

I wandered around for a while, the wind kicking up dirt, until I came to a little worn-out brick building with *The Paisano* painted on the side. I walked up the crumbling steps and pulled open the door. Inside, everything smelled like rotted wood and formaldehyde. An elk's head hung from the far wall. A baby grand stood in the corner of the room, unplayable. Behind the counter was a dwarf of a woman wearing a floral dress and sporting a rowdy blue bouffant. She had pasty white skin, cherub cheeks, and a turkey wattle. She put away the flask she'd been sipping from and stuck it beneath the counter. Then she looked up at me and smiled through gritted teeth, revulsion concealed. How can I help you, mister? she said.

I want a room.

Just a room? Or will there be something else? She said this with no playfulness.

Only a room.

Okay, she said. I can get you a room. She reached behind the counter and grabbed a key.

I followed her up a narrow flight of stairs, the lightbulb dangling from the ceiling creating menacing shadows.

The second floor was in bad shape. Paint peeling from the ceiling, curling up on itself, lights flickering, walls covered with graffiti, gibberish all. From inside one of the rooms, I could hear somebody moaning. Against one wall there was a wooden bench, and sitting on the bench was a young woman wearing red boots and a red wig and a badly tattered wedding dress. A cigarette dangled from a lipstick-smeared mouth. She winked at me and I looked away. Ugly face, she said. Don't bother me none. I'll suck your cock.

You keep that pie-hole shut, the hotel owner said. Now git on back to your room. C'mon, git!

The girl rolled her eyes and rose to her feet. She rearranged her underwear and slunk on down the hallway. With a smile or a sneer, she opened a door and disappeared to the dull gray light of a T.V. show.

Don't mind her, the blue-haired woman said. With a violent jerk she pulled open a jammed room door and handed me the key. Well, I sure do hope you enjoy your stay, she said. She studied my corroded features for a moment, her amblyopic eye drifting toward her skull. And if you need anything, don't hesitate to ask.

I won't need anything, I said.

*   *   *

The room was what you might expect. Grime-scrubbed walls. A sloppily made bed. An old Kelvinator refrigerator with the kickplate ajar. A filthy window overlooking a filthy town.

I sat down on the bed and removed my jacket and my boots. I unzipped my bag and pulled out a can of George W. Helme snuff, a bottle of plum brandy, an army-issued bayonet, and my worn leather King James Bible, the pages starting to yellow.

I snorted some tobacco, took a long pull of burnt wine, and opened the Bible: *And Gideon said unto him, Oh my Lord, if the LORD be with us, why then is all this befallen us? and where be all his miracles which our fathers told us of, saying, Did not the LORD bring us up from Egypt? but now the LORD hath forsaken us, and delivered us into the hands of the Midianites...*

The power of the passage moved me, and I collapsed on the bed, eyes squeezed tight. I was beginning to think that there wasn't a single righteous person in the world. I was beginning to think that everybody had secrets, terrible secrets.

*   *   *

That night I lay in my bed, bonnell coils jabbing my skin, and stared at the mildewed ceiling. There was a long, jagged crack. I watched it grow. Water dripped from the crack into a rusted pot. Drip, drip, drip. Chinese water torture. Through narrow slits, I gazed out the window. The moon was the color of jaundiced skin.

I couldn't sleep at all. The mice and rats had taken over the house. I could hear them scurrying along the wooden floors, climbing up the walls, gnawing at the furniture. And then I heard something else. The faint echo of footsteps on the pavement down below. I crawled out of bed and stared out the window. A man walked slowly down the street, just out of the glow of the streetlight. He wore a tattered suit, a blue tie hanging around his neck like a noose. He had iron-gray hair, badly disheveled, a skeletal frame, and a haunted, emaciated face. When he saw my silhouette in the window, he froze and stared right at me. I shivered involuntarily. A lunatic smile spread slowly across his face. I took a couple of steps backward, my breath trapped in my windpipe…

*   *   *

An hour or more passed. I sat in the bed clutching my knife. Every so often I'd take a peek outside. He hadn't moved; he just stood there, waiting. The wind was blowing, the rain was falling, and a screen door was slamming open and shut.

*   *   *

12:05 A.M., and I heard a knocking on the door. Three short knocks. I gripped my bayonet tightly. I walked slowly across the room, sinews full of dread. I unlocked the door and pulled it open. Dull light spread across the hardwood floor, and I shielded my eyes with my hand. But it wasn't the stranger. It was the redhead from the bar, her face all blurry, a rain-soaked windshield.

I know it's late, she said in a little girl's voice.

I wasn't sleeping.

Can I come inside?

I'm not gonna stop you.

She smiled that crooked smile and stepped into the room, the door slamming shut behind her. She wore a red Nancy Drew raincoat tied tightly at the waist. I was wearing boxers with bears on them and an A-frame undershirt. She looked me up and down. You're well-built, she said. I don't mind the face. I've seen worse.

Maybe, I said. Do you want something to drink? I have plum brandy. Don't have any glasses, though.

Well, that would be just fine, she said. Do you mind if I take off my jacket?

No, ma'am.

She wasn't wearing much underneath. Just a futuristic-looking little silver dress and the same red boots as before. I handed her the bottle of brandy and she took a nice long swig, watching me from the corner of her eyes. She was a drunk, a bad girl, but she reminded me of somebody from long ago...

I wanted to thank you, she said, for how you helped me this afternoon. Most men would have walked away.

I shrugged my shoulders. The way I was raised, a fellow's not supposed to lay a hand on a woman. And if he does, you're supposed to do something about it. Who was he?

She took another swig, this one longer than the first, and wiped her mouth with the back of her hand.

My husband, she said.

I nodded. And you gonna stay with him?

Probably.

I said: A guy hits you once, he'll hit you twice.

Oh, he's hit me more than twice, believe me. You didn't see anything today. She stared at me for a long moment, then pulled up her sleeve and showed me the remnants of a couple of cigar burns.

I clenched my jaw and shook my head. You ought to leave him, I said.

It's not so simple.

Sure it is. You pack up your bags. And you leave. Simple.

She didn't say anything for a while. Then: This brandy sure is good. I've never had brandy before.

Yeah. I like it okay.

For the next hour or so we drank the brandy and smoked cigarettes. I'd stopped thinking about the stranger, stopped thinking about the Mountain. Off in the distance calliope music was playing. The girl touched my leg with her hand. Her skin was soft, her fingernails filthy. She licked the corner of her mouth, said, And Joseph? Do you think I'm pretty, just a little?

Yes, I lied. I think you're very pretty.

Well, then?

She moved closer on the bed. Her face was in soft focus. Pimpled skin. Bloodshot eyes. Lovely, no. But I was in love. It happens too easily for me.

She placed her hand on mine and moved it beneath her dress. The calliope music got louder. I was feeling good and anxious. There were some things I wanted to do. I wanted to howl at the moon, I wanted to knock her around. But I was paralyzed. She leaned in close. I could smell the layers of perfume and sweat and burnt wine. Her mouth smiled against my skin.

I pulled her toward me. A dog barked spastically. I placed my hand between her thighs. She moaned. A familiar revulsion spread through my veins. I felt like I was going to be sick. Maybe we shouldn't do this, I said. Maybe it isn't right.

She grinned, baring her fangs. For how long have you been concerned about right and wrong?

I thought that one over for a moment. Then I grabbed her by the hand and pulled her to her feet. With a quick jerk, I shoved her against the wall. She gasped, but the smile never left her face. I studied her eyes. I could've found the truth, maybe, but I didn't want to. Instead, I reached back and slapped her across the face, got her attention. Then I kissed her hard, biting down on her lower lip until it bled.

*   *   *

There's not much more to tell. She let me do some things. I couldn't stop myself. When we were done, she told me we might fall in love.

I don't even know your name, I said.

Lilith, she said. Created from clay...

After that we lay in bed for a while without talking. Outside, the wind kicked a tin can down the sidewalk and I felt good and empty. I squeezed my eyes shut and fell asleep. I dreamed that old familiar dream: a murder of crows, circling over a mining shack, cawing in excitement, and me being pinned down by faceless demons...

When I woke, the sun was rising and the sky was a bloody mess. My body was drenched with ethanol sweat. I sat up, head aching but good. Lilith was lying on her side, head propped up on the palm of her hand. A sly grin on her face.

So? Did you have fun, Joseph?

Well, sure.

Just so you know, I don't usually do this kind of thing.

No. I'm sure you don't.

I'm not that kind of a girl. Not usually.

She lit a cigarette and sucked down the smoke, eyes unblinking. And then the question. Unspoken usually. Not with Lilith. No transition even. Your face, Joseph. The scars. What happened? I know I shouldn't ask, but...

I met her gaze for a moment and then shook my head. It's okay, I said. I reached across her body and grabbed the package of cigarettes. I stuck one in my mouth but didn't light it. It bounced up and down as I spoke. I told her the story. I knew the story well.

I was in the Marine Corps, I said. 1st Battalion, 7th Regiment, 1st Division. Stationed in Mosul. Bank of the Tigris. Home of Jonah. Home of Nahum. To me it was hell on Earth. I hadn't been there long, not more than two months. I was with my unit and we were driving in a Humvee. We were trying to secure the area or hunt for insurgents or build a nation. It doesn't matter. Anyway, we were driving down this dirt road and it was pitch black, and our lights were off. We were wearing night vision goggles, so we could see. We came to this tiny bridge over a canal.

Nobody was worried, soldiers were joking around, talking about whores they'd screwed and towel-heads they'd killed. We drove across the bridge and suddenly I got this bad feeling. I don't know why, can't explain it. It wasn't a moment later when we hit the tripwire. They got us but good. My eardrums exploded and the world went up in flames.

The Humvee finally came to a stop. I could tell I was torn up pretty good but I didn't feel any pain. Flames were everywhere. Then I heard my squad leader screaming: I think I lost my leg! Oh, Jesus, I think I lost my leg! And my best friend Dan was in the front passenger seat where the bomb went off and he was screaming: Where's help? Where the fuck is help? And then everything went quiet.

Time passed in a dream sequence. Everything was out of order and mixed up. I saw trucks materialize through the dust and flames. And then a soldier with a gas mask. His head was jerking all over the place in a strobe light. He disappeared and the flames got stronger, hotter. Then he reappeared and I saw him crawling into the Humvee, sticking out his hand. I guess he saved me. I never saw him again.

Next thing I knew, I was lying on the dirt and my whole body was burning and throbbing and I tried to cry but I couldn't. I reached for my face and it was all swollen on one side, and when I touched it, my middle finger went deep into my temple. Everything started getting blurry. I closed my eyes.

I heard voices loud and panicked and incoherent. They thought I was a goner. I wanted to open my eyes, wanted to say something, but I had no control.

The world ended for a time. The next thing I remember is being in a chopper, flying over the burning desert, and I wasn't sure if I was dead or not and I prayed to God that I was. And then I drifted away again and I don't remember anything else until I got to the hospital...

I stopped talking and looked over at Lilith. Her shoulders were trembling and her eyes were moist. She touched my cheek with what might have been tenderness.

I guess I'd told the story well.

CHAPTER 3

The next morning, I got my car towed. The day was cold and windy, the sun a dull flash in a gunmetal sky. The shop was nothing but a little brick building with the words *Auto Repair* written in big block letters. It was squeezed between a dilapidated food market called Charlie's and a derelict church, its bell rusted into a permanent slant.

In the front lot there were all sorts of oddities: a rotted canoe, a covered wagon, an open coffin. There were hubcaps and unicycles and antique gas pumps. There were mangled jalopies and rusted car parts. A young guy with slicked-back rockabilly hair sat on a metal bench in front of the office. His face and hands and overalls were covered in filth; he looked like a Vaudeville performer in black face. He was smoking a short stogie and drinking a Squirt. He didn't seem happy to see me.

Having some problems? he said. He had a smiling skull ring on his middle finger and dried spittle in the corner of his mouth.

It's an old Chevy C30, I said. Never had a problem before. And now it just stopped driving. Let me down big-time. Think you can fix it?

He flashed a tobacco-stained smile. Gimme a tool set and I could fix Venus de Milo. If this here truck can be fixed, I'm the one who can do it. Good thing you didn't take her to Paul's. He wouldn't know the difference between a V8 engine and V8 drink. He's ruptured more piston seals than I've screwed horny housewives.

Is that a lot?

Hell yeah, that's a lot!

He farmer-blew some snot onto the ground before getting into the truck. With the door flung open, he turned the ignition a couple of times and shook his head. Then he got out and looked under the hood and spat. When was the last time you had this thing worked on? he said.

I shrugged my shoulders. Been a while, I said. It's not my car. The car belongs to a friend. He lent it to me.

Ain't a drop of oil left, that's one problem. But it ain't your only. Have a seat in that there office, and I'll take a look, give you an estimate. I'm fair, too, not like Paul. He'd overcharge a goddamn beggar, yes he would.

For the next hour or more, I sat inside the dingy little store reading *Motor Trend* and *Playboy* and drinking cold coffee while Hal took apart the pickup piece by piece. I could hear him cursing and complaining and mumbling under his breath. Finally, the glass door slammed open and Hal entered, wiping perspiration from his forehead with a rag. His lips were tugged into a frown, his eyes darting all over the place.

She can't be fixed, Hal said, his bedside manner lacking.

What do you mean she can't be fixed?

I mean, the old girl is ready for the junkyard. She ain't got another mile in her. You got a hole in the cylinder. The piston rings are completely worn down. The crankshaft ain't turning. And that's just for starters.

I thought you said you could fix any vehicle.

That ain't what I said. I said I could fix her, *if* she could be fixed. This one can't be fixed. I'd have to replace the engine completely. Ain't worth your time or trouble. You'd be better served junking this one and buying another. There's a few used-car lots down on North Main.

I'm not interested in another truck, I said. This is a good truck. I drove it all the way across the country. She hasn't failed me yet. She can be fixed. I know she can be fixed.

He reached into his pocket and pulled out an oversized pinch of leaf tobacco and stuck it into his mouth. He spat on the floor and said: Like I said, I'd have to replace the engine. It would cost you a lot of money.

How much?

A new complete engine would cost you two grand at least. A salvage yard one might cost up to a grand. Add another five hundred for the work. You could buy a brand-new used truck for not much more than that.

I stuffed my hands in my pockets and kicked at the dirt. I thought things over for a few moments. Put in a salvage yard engine, I said. Be sure it's a good one. I need to make it up to the Mountain. There's somebody waiting for me.

Whatever you say, boss. It's your money.

How soon can you have it done?

Gimme four, five days, top, he said. Got a number where I can call you?

I shook my head. I'll just come back in five days, I said. It's a good truck.

And I started walking.

* * *

I made my way back to town, along dirt roads lined with rotted mailboxes and sad-luck houses. The wind blew through the skeleton trees and everything smelled like a feedlot. My hands were buried in my pockets. I was thinking ugly thoughts. You know the kind. Death and destruction. I walked past rusted metal barrels and mounds of used tires and rows of dying alfalfa, but no humans. The sky was the color of bone. Down about a quarter of a mile, I came upon a cemetery that hadn't been cared for in years. Dignity denied in both life and death.

In the middle of town, on top of Jagged Hill, stood The Church of Sacred Blood, a white-spire structure with a mural of Christ surrounded by drunken angels, the wooden cross weary, hanging on for dear life. A preacher's voice echoed across the plains: *And you have heard it said that as you walk through the valley of the shadow of death you shall fear no evil, for he is with you; his rod and staff comforts you. But I say to you: Be afraid. Because the Lord does not want any whores and bastards. The Lord does not want any thieves and beggars. The Lord desires the righteous. And how many of you are righteous? Well? How many? Hell awaits you. Yes, my friends, hell surely awaits unless some changes are made. For you are nothing but maggots and cockroaches, a blight in the Lord's eye. And there is time for conversion, for restoration, but time is running thin...*

I made my way along a broken path until I came to my hotel, all marked by sorry dilapidation and decay. Breathing heavily, I leaned against the brick wall and yanked out a cigarette. I sucked in the smoke slow and tender and spat it out fast and mean.

And that's when I saw the stranger.

He was a block ahead, wearing the same tattered suit as before. His face was in the shadows, but I could tell it was him. The wind was blowing, and a few specks of snow were swirling above, never seeming to land. I pulled up the collar of my jacket and started walking down the splintered pavement, past a slumbering Mexican clutching a bottle of Sauza, past an elderly woman walking her vacuum cleaner, past a mangy calico cat gnawing on a piece of rotting flesh. The stranger must have seen me too: he started walking, following after me.

My slow gait changing to a gallop, I made my way down the street and then ducked into an alleyway. There were broken bottles and bloodied underwear and seagulls lost from the landfill. There was a wild-looking old woman with splayed gray hair and

Corrosion

a whale skin jacket, trying to light a fire in a trash can. When she saw me, she charged toward me and started pounding open-fisted on my back. She was shouting about satellites and wiretaps and port-a-potties. She smelled like mothballs and soda fizz. I pushed away from her and spun into the service entrance of one of the dilapidated buildings. The door shut behind me, and everything was dark. It took me several moments before my eyes adjusted. There were dozens of empty plastic crates. There was also a darkened staircase. I walked up the staircase slowly, the wooden steps moaning beneath my feet.

At the top of the steps was a metal door, dull light shining from beneath it. I turned the handle and pushed open the door. I walked into a strange room with strange shadows and strange people. It took me a while to recognize that they were mannequins and I was inside some sort of a defunct clothing store…

I just stood there for a while. Everything was quiet. I looked around the room. There were dozens of boxes stuffed messily with clothes. Blow-out signs on the wall. Somebody had been in a hurry to leave the business behind. There was a cash register on the counter, open and empty. I squatted down on the floor, breathing heavily. Outside I could hear the crazy woman singing a strange gypsy tune:

Oh child, oh child,
Where have you gone?
You done gone missing
Two dolls left on the lawn

I sat in that clothing store for a long time. The stranger never found me. When I finally left, the sky was black and the moon was missing.

CHAPTER 4

Over the next several days, I saw a lot of Lilith. We always met in the Hotel Paisano and she was never all that discrete. She came in through the front door and left the same way, and the townspeople whispered behind their hands. I asked wasn't she worried about her husband finding out but she just acted tough. Serve that bastard right, she said. How many whores has he screwed?

During these times we talked some, but I got to know Lilith less than you might think. I couldn't quite figure her out. Sometimes she could be soft and motherly, stroking my forehead and telling me that everything would be okay; other times she'd seem hard and cruel, making acerbic comments about my service, my intelligence. Then when she'd see the anger in my eyes, she'd apologize and shift back to sweetness.

Not only that, but her appearance was always changing, too. One day she'd wear a tight leather miniskirt reaching halfway down her thigh, the next a white dress covering her ankles, arms, and neck. She dyed her hair from red to platinum blonde, and even changed the color of her eyes — from brown to Jolly Rancher blue.

One thing she was consistent about was her feelings for her husband. Fear and loathing. She'd only married him because she'd got pregnant and was scared. She'd lost the baby and kept the monster. He could be charming, but not all that often. She showed me the bruises and the cigar burns. Told me about when he'd broken her jaw, when he'd given her a black eye.

I was beginning to think their marriage wouldn't last.

*   *   *

This one morning Lilith was in the bathroom sitting on the toilet. I was lying in bed, running my finger along my facial scars, watching her intently in the mirror. Her red knees were touching, her panties around her ankles, and a wounded cigarette was hanging from her lips. She rose to her feet, wiped herself off, and flushed the toilet. Hunching over, she inserted a tampon with one hand, the cigarette now burning in the other. She returned to the bedroom and slumped down in a chair. She was too skinny. I'd never seen her eat.

Oh, Joseph, she said. I'm so fucking tired of being afraid. It's wearing me down. It gets so I can't ever sleep and my stomach is always aching.

You worrying about Nick?

She nodded her head. You have no idea what it's like, living in fear all the time.

I have some sense.

He makes my skin crawl. You just have no fucking idea.

Couldn't you just divorce him? I said.

Lilith scowled and glared at me. Her bleached hair was a mess and her eyes were bloodshot. She took a long drag from her cigarette and let the smoke trickle out of her nostrils. Divorce him, huh?

Well, sure.

He'd kill me if I ever left him, she said.

What are you talking about?

That's what he told me. Said he'd slit my throat and dump me in the landfill.

He talks tough, I said. A lot of guys talk tough.

I believe him, she said.

I shook my head. He doesn't have it in him. I know his type. He's a bully, but he's not a killer. It takes courage to kill.

She sucked a burning house full of smoke into her lungs and blew it out of a Billy Idol mouth. Then her face softened and her lips curled into a smile. Without saying a word, she rose from the chair and walked slowly, seductively to the bed. She sat down next to me and started stroking my chest, her left breast pressing against my skin, and for a moment I decided that I would place my fate in her sloppily manicured hands.

When I spoke again, it sounded like somebody else's voice, all cracked and distant: We could run away, I said. Just you and me. Leave all of this behind, you know? I have a little place in the mountains, not two hours from here, just a little mining cabin buried in a thatch of trees. Nobody within two miles in any direction. That's where I was going when my car broke down. I was going to the Mountain. Just to get away from everything. Just to clear my mind. We could go there. We could be happy, maybe.

Lilith sucked down some more smoke, her eyes narrowing to a pair of gashes. Oh, that sounds nice, she said. I've never been to the mountains. But he'd find me. I know he would.

Not up there, I said. Not a person in the world would find you.

Then I pulled her close and kissed her, mashing my lips against hers. Lilith closed her eyes and covered her fluttering heart with the palm of her hand. But it was no good. A fellow can get so goddamn lonely sometimes...

*   *   *

Lilith was going to spend the day with an aunt in Rifle. Me, I had nothing planned. I figured what the hell. I'd go pay Nick McClellan a visit.

The McClellans lived a few miles outside of town. I walked part of the way. Then I stuck out my thumb and got lucky. An old blue Lincoln Continental pulled off the side of the road, kicking up dust. I jogged up to the car and the passenger-side door opened. Inside was an older man with thick gray muttonchops and friendly blue eyes. Where you headed, mister? No visible reaction to my face.

Just up the road a bit, I said.

Hop in.

His name was Big Ed. He chewed tobacco but never spat. His fingers tapped the steering wheel incessantly, keeping time with the wheels on the highway. And he must have been afraid of silence.

Me, I'm on my way to work, he said. Wanna know what I do? I shrugged my shoulders. He chuckled a bit. Then he said: I clean out Porta-Potties. Damn straight. Spend my days in them outhouses, sucking up shit with a wand. Fellow can't complain, though. Gotta make a living, right? Beats living under the bridge. Done that too. Shit. And what about you? Got a trade?

No, I said. Not really.

A drifter, huh?

Veteran. Iraq.

Well, shit, I kinda figured, you know. Vietnam, myself. Got a bullet lodged in my ass. God's honest truth. Nothing like your injury, though. That's a hell of a thing. IED?

Yes, sir.

Say no more, soldier. You've probably relived it enough.

Yes. I guess I have.

He rolled down the window and the wind whipped in the car. You said Army, right? he said.

No, sir. Marines.

A big grin spread across his face. No shit? He pulled up his sleeve and showed me his skull-and-sword tattoo. Proud member myself, he said. Mind if I ask you a question?

No, sir.

Ed stuck his fingers in his mouth and pulled out the damp wad of chewing tobacco and threw it outside. How they been treating you?

Sir?

Since you got back to the States. You been treated with respect?

Yes, sir, I said. I have no complaints, sir.

Must have been tough on your family, though. What with your injuries and all.

My parents died a long time ago, I said. I got no friends, no family.

He nodded his head for so long I wasn't sure he'd ever stop. When he spoke again, his words were drenched with bitterness: You know, they used to hold a parade for all of us soldiers in this here town. People lined Main Street, held their children on their shoulders, waved their American flags, played patriotic marches. But the years went by and the parades became smaller and smaller. Fewer veterans. Fewer townspeople. Finally, one year I noticed that it was just me. No more bands playing. No more children cheering. No more women weeping. Just me. I saw a fellow who I recognized from the war. He asked me what did I think I was doing still marching. And I said, It's our duty. And he said, Nobody's doing it anymore. And I said, As long as I'm doing it, somebody's doing it.

Then Ed stopped talking. There was no moral to the story.

We finally came to the McClellan property, way out in the middle of nowhere, surrounded by dirt and dust and derricks and devils. Ed stopped the car and jerked it into park. He looked at me for a good long while, making me uncomfortable. I go to this group, he said. Once a week. Veterans. All kinds. Vietnam, Kuwait, Iraq, Afghanistan. Hell, we even got an old-timer from Korea. It's good to be able to talk. Helps exorcise them demons, you know? If you keep it all inside of you... Anyway, we meet Wednesdays at seven. Down at the American Legion. The way I figure, ain't nobody can understand a soldier like a soldier.

I nodded my head slowly. I sure do appreciate the offer, I said, but I'm not all that interested.

No?

It's just that I don't much like talking about the past. It always seems to be changing on me.

He looked at me some more. Then he stuck out his hand and I shook it. Been a pleasure, soldier, he said.

Thanks for the ride, I said. I'd just opened the door and stepped outside when he spoke again, a big grin spread across his face: Good night, Chesty Puller, wherever you are!

I didn't know what he was talking about. Who's Chesty Puller? I said.

Something set him off. His expression changed to a scowl and he started cursing at me. Before I could get an explanation, he jammed the truck into drive and sped off down the road.

*   *   *

Outside, it was cold and breezy and the ground was covered with frost. I gazed at the McClellans' house, a little brick ranch, maybe 1,000 square feet big. An American flag hung out front, whipping in the wind. Behind the house were a bunch of cylindrical feed bins alongside a pair of wood barns, both bigger than the house. I peeked in the first barn. It was lined with narrow stalls made of concrete. Sows sat inside, pregnant, eating from the feeders that hung above the stalls.

I made my way to the house, not sure what I aimed to do. On the porch, the wind chimes were jingling, playing a madman's orchestra. I rapped on the door a few times. No answer. I moved toward the window and peered in the house. Didn't look like anybody was home. I tried the door. It was unlocked. I stepped inside.

The home was simple. In the living room there was a ratty couch and a television. There was an Oriental rug on the floor and a pair of boots by the door. The walls were bare except for a metal cross above the couch.

I made my way to the bedroom. The curtains were shut and everything was dark and drab. The bed was unmade. Clothes were strewn on the hardwood floor. There was another television sitting on a wooden crate. The white dresser looked antique. Some of the drawers were sticking out. On top of the dresser were a couple of bowling trophies.

Next, I wandered to the kitchen. Dishes were piling up in the sink. The floral wallpaper was peeling from the walls. I opened the refrigerator and grabbed a beer. I returned to the living room, sat down on the couch, and crossed my legs. Some time passed. I didn't move. I just stared at the wall thinking about everything and nothing at all.

I slammed down the beer and crushed the can with my hand. Then I tossed it on the floor.

I stayed like that on the couch for another twenty minutes at least. Nick didn't show up. I don't know what I would have done if he had. I rose to my feet and walked out of the brick ranch, letting the screen door slam shut behind me.

Once outside, I met up with one of his pigs. And here's what I did, here's exactly what I did: I grabbed that hog from behind, pulled out my knife, and sliced its throat from one end to the other. Then I stood over him, watching him twitch and moan. I waited until he had bled out and dragged him back to the front porch. That would give ol' Nick something to think about...

CHAPTER 5

The next morning I went back to Hal's Auto. He was under the hood of an old VW Bug. Bob Miller was singing from a plastic radio. The air was cold and my hands were buried in my pockets.

I stood there tapping my feet and humming with the radio, but he just kept right on working. So I stood next to him, leaned under the hood and said, I'm looking for my pickup. She ready yet?

He looked up with that vaudeville face, flashed his milk-white teeth, and said, C30 with the blown engine, right?

Yes, sir.

He straightened up and wiped his hands on his jeans. Sure, I got her fixed, he said. Found a nice little engine at the junkyard. Got plenty of juice in her, too. Came from an old hearse. That doesn't bother you now, does it?

No, sir. Not as long as my truck runs.

She runs like a dream. Course I can't vouch for the longevity.

The pickup was parked next to Hal's office. He'd washed and cleaned her, and she looked as good as new. He popped open the hood and pointed out various intricacies, but I wasn't much interested.

How much do I owe you? I said.

He pulled out a pad and pencil and scribbled a few things down. 596 for the engine, he said. 480 for labor. I'll give you the stranger's discount, and we'll make it an even grand.

Fine, I said. I'll pay cash.

And pay cash I did. I got into the truck, hit the corpse engine and drove on out of the parking lot.

*   *   *

Broken-down cars, hotel rooms, booze—it was beginning to take its toll on me financially. The truth was, I was down to less than a hundred dollars. I sold blood and an old watch. Not enough to make a difference. Eventually I was forced to get a job. After a few days of searching, I found one at the local landfill. Twelve twenty-five an hour. The job wasn't much, but at this particular time, as I dangled from a window ledge, it suited me just fine. I figured the Mountain could wait, and besides I liked Lilith more than plenty.

My boss's name was Cash Hopkins and he was some slave driver. He was a little guy, couldn't have been more than five foot six, with ashen gray hair and a complexion to match. He was fifty or sixty or seventy. He never stopped shouting. Move that god-damn refuse! he'd shout. There are a thousand wet-backs chomping at the bit to take your job!

The job was monotonous. Every thirty or so min-utes a garbage truck would appear over the hill, per-form a pirouette, and spill a load of crushed trash. Then the bulldozers would race toward the last dump, lower their blades, and shove all the waste to-ward the middle, a never-ending task of efficiency. They refused to train me on the bulldozer, despite my experience driving an M-1A1 Abrams tank. In-stead they gave me a shovel. I did the best I could, moving trash and scaring away crows.

And so there I was this one particular morning, standing on top of the world, and all around me was trash and filth, and I knew there was some greater truth but I couldn't figure out what it was. I stood there perfectly still just thinking, thinking, thinking. The moon was a silver disc in the pale blue sky. Ev-erything was quiet; the bulldozers were on the other side of the hill. I waded through the sea of debris, sucking in the rotten air. The crows hovered cautious-ly overhead. Suddenly I was overcome with emotion. I fell to my knees, became engulfed in garbage. And I prayed with all my might. Jesus, I really need a hand. I'm afraid I'm ready to really fuck things up again…

And it was at that moment that the stranger ap-peared, his figure silhouetted by sunshine. I strug-gled to my feet, using my shovel as a cane. A crow landed on his shoulder, cocked its head and flew away. He walked toward me slowly, his left leg drag-ging behind his right.

He stood in front of me, just staring at me with

contempt. His face was unshaven and his eyes were vengeful. There were spider veins crawling up his cheeks. His gray hair was greasy and unkempt. When he spoke, his voice was all full of pebbles: Who are you, he said, only it didn't really seem to be a question.

I met his gaze. I think I should be asking you the same question.

I been following you around, he said, rocking back and forth, just watching you.

I've seen you. Should've called the cops. Didn't. Sometimes you're not an easy man to keep track of. But I always find you. After a while.

He had a strange way of talking. He paused at odd times. His voice trembled slightly.

What do you want? I said. Why are you following me?

He took a couple of steps forward. My body tensed. I could feel my knife resting beneath my shirt. There was nobody else around...

My son saw terrible things, he said. Roadside bombs. Firing squads. The night sky on fire. Heads severed from torsos, staring back at him blinking slowly...

What are you talking about? I said.

His cheek twitched and his eyes narrowed. I searched his face, trying to recall a past life...

You claim to be a soldier, he said. Isn't that right?

Yes, sir. 1st Battalion, 7th Regiment, 1st Division. Honorable discharge.

He stared at me for a long time. Then he started laughing. Only it wasn't a happy laughter. It was awful, terrified laughter.

43

I read about you, he said. In a newspaper. In Lubbock.

I know the article.

Said you were wounded in Mosul. Were you wounded in Mosul?

I nodded my head. Yes, sir. I was.

Said you'd had a tough time of it since returning to the States. What with your face and all. Nobody would hire you. You were homeless for a time.

I've never felt sorry for myself, I said. Not for a single moment.

He moved forward until he was inches from my face. I felt threatened. I pulled out my knife and showed it to him up close. He smiled that sickly smile. What are you gonna do? he said. You gonna kill me?

Just move back, I said. I don't know who you are but—

I lost concentration. He lunged at me and grabbed a hold of my wrist. The knife clattered to the ground. I tried reaching for it, and when I was off-balance, he shoved me hard, causing me to tumble into a pile of trash. He picked up the knife and squatted down next to me. His face now looked hard and mean.

You ever seen me before? he said.

I shook my head.

I said, you ever seen me before?

No, sir.

You say your name is Joseph Downs, huh? Iraqi veteran, huh?

Yes.

Tell me your unit.

I already told you.

44

Tell it to me again. This time he was shouting.

1st Battalion, 7th Regiment, 1st Division. What the hell is this?

When did you serve?

What?

Dates served, soldier! He pressed the knife against my throat, drawing a trickle of blood.

Shipped out August 11, 2004, I said. Honorable discharge…May 13, 2005.

Bullshit! he shouted. Who are you?

I already told you, I said. Jesus, what is wrong with you? What do you want from me? I can show you my tag—I keep it around my neck.

His eyes opened wide and his lower lip trembled. Give it to me, he said. Let me see your tag.

Put the knife down, I said.

Slowly, he placed the knife on the ground, inches from his body. He nodded his head. I removed the tag from around my neck and tossed it gently toward him. He picked it up without taking his eyes off me.

DOWNS

J.D.

522715386

USMC M

BAPTIST

He stared down at that tag for some time. Then his jaw slackened and his eyes filled with dread. He shook his head a few times and muttered something under his breath. He dropped the tag on the ground and then grabbed a shovel to steady himself.

He continued muttering but I couldn't decipher the words.

Uneasily, I rose to my feet and backed away. Listen, I said. I'm not looking for any trouble. I was on my way to the Mountain when my car broke down. There's been a misunderstanding of some kind.

The stranger looked at me wild-eyed. I'm not crazy, he said. I'm not crazy. He backed away slowly. I'm not crazy! Then he turned and lurched forward like a wounded animal. I watched as he dissolved into the trash around him. And as a fleet of garbage trucks appeared over the horizon, I wondered if he had really been there at all…

CHAPTER 6

There was this one fellow I worked with. Dustin Fender was his name. Usually he was on the bull-dozer, but occasionally he'd be on slop duty with me, shoveling refuse. He had a muscular build and a Ne-anderthal face. He liked to tell stories; most of them were lies. He claimed that he'd survived a jet crash, set the Wyoming record for clean-jerk, fathered a dozen illegitimate children. He was a nice enough fellow and he liked to drink plenty. Every evening after work you could find him at a highway road-house called The Watering Hole sucking down gaso-line, talking about the old days.

On this particular afternoon he was lounging on a vomit-damaged couch, smoking a cigarette down to the filter. Me, I was busy working like a son-of-a-bitch. Sweat was dripping down my forehead and landing in my eyes. Damn, boy, he said. You work too hard.

I wiped off my forehead with the crook of my arm. Just my nature, I said. Learned it from my old man. Besides. Hard work never hurt anybody.

Dustin killed his cigarette and grinned. Shit. Why take chances?

I gripped the shovel tighter. You ought to spend some time in boot camp, I said. Then you'd learn a thing or two about hard work. The sergeant used to wake us up at three in the morning, make us do fifty pushups, tell us to go back to sleep. Then he'd come in twenty minutes later and tell us to run a mile in the muck and mire. And if every last one of us couldn't do it in under seven minutes, he'd make us strip our clothes and lie on the floor and he'd just start kicking us with those steel boots until we were bleeding and puking and shitting.

Goddamn, that don't seem right.

You wouldn't get it, I said. The toughness that's needed to be a soldier. You just wouldn't get it.

Yeah. I guess not, he said. He rose to his feet, stuck a handful of Hot Tamales into his mouth, and stuffed the box back into his shirt pocket. Then he glanced at his watch. Four thirty. What you say we duck out of here a little early?

Well, I don't know…

Come on. It's just a half an hour. The trash will still be here tomorrow. Christ, there'll be even more of it. We could grab a drink or two.

I shrugged my shoulders. Yeah, sure, why not? It's been a long week. It's been a long life.

*   *   *

The Watering Hole was located out on Highway 52 right across from the rendering plant. The bar was in bad shape. The linoleum floor was warped and so were the walls. The wooden chairs were rotting, a couple of them lying dead on the floor. The jukebox was playing Tammy Wynette, but it was too slow and she sounded like Johnny Cash. There was an old man sitting at the bar with a bottle of bourbon and a wooden cane. Around his neck hung a sign: *My name is John Holton. I suffer from Alzheimer's Disease. I live at 42 Steele Street.* There were several Mexicans from the rendering plant still in white uniforms and hard hats. In the middle of the bar, a fat man was spinning a fatter woman round and round. She was laughing hysterically, her breasts jiggling like Jell-O. Dustin said: It ain't the Taj Mahal, but they serve good whiskey.

We sat down at the bar and he ordered a couple of Jim Beams and Budweisers. The barmaid was a skinny lady with spaghetti blonde hair. She must have known Dustin pretty well because she didn't mind when he accidentally/on purpose touched her left tit while reaching for his drinks. You're a naughty boy, she said. Then: Who's your friend?

This here is Joseph Downs, he said, an Iraqi war veteran, and the finest shovel man at the landfill.

She smiled at my burnt face and stuck out her slender hand. Pleasure to meet you, Joseph. Army? Navy?

Marine, I said. 1st Battalion, 7th Regiment, 1st Division. Stationed in Mosul. Still have scars on my face and sand in my lungs.

How exciting.

I shook my head. Wouldn't call it exciting. I saw

terrible things. I saw men come apart from their limbs and heads and souls. I saw children mangled beyond recognition. I saw Christ's lonely hand reaching out from beneath a ton of rubble.

Dustin laughed and patted my back. Hell of a guy, ain't he? Fucking war hero!

The barmaid nodded her head and smiled. Yes. Yes, he is.

*   *   *

Dustin and I played shuffleboard. He was better than me. He kept buying me drinks. An hour passed, then another. We destroyed a pint of booze, maybe more. He told me more lies and I ate them up. I liked this Dustin. I liked the way I was feeling. I decided that I would start drinking more often.

And that's when I saw her. Lilith. My little hellcat. She came crashing into the bar, a roller-coaster grin on her face, a gangly Mexican on her arm. He wore a black cowboy hat and a black mustache: a real *vaquero*. She wore a rhinestone-studded Western snap shirt, tight blue jeans, and pink cowgirl boots with tassels and silver stars. Her hair was still blonde, but there were fresh streaks of black. From the way she was slurring her speech, I figured she'd been to a bar or two before this one. They were getting plenty friendly with each other. She waved down the bartender and whispered something into the *vaquero's* ear and they both laughed. I stayed in the shadows drinking Yukon Jack and thinking, thinking.

They sat at the bar for a while and had a hell of a time. He kept trying to kiss her and she didn't do much to stop him. Meanwhile, Dustin kept talking and laughing. My head was full of unpleasant thoughts. I drank more.

I didn't know what to do. I thought about confronting the *vaquero*. I thought about confronting Lilith. I didn't. I didn't do anything at all.

They didn't stay too long. Just long enough for a few drinks, just long enough for Lilith to dance sloppily to a Dwight Yoakam song before collapsing to the floor like a broken marionette. When they left, she was dry heaving and the *vaquero* was screaming out a *grito Mexicano*: AY YA YAY YA!

As for me, I wasn't feeling good at all. I stumbled toward the back of the bar, blood trickling from my right nostril. Inside the bathroom everything was mixed up. The sinks were spilling whiskey, the urinals were upside down, and rats were crawling on the ceiling. I stared into the mirror. It was cracked badly and my face was a Picasso painting, parts everywhere. I slicked back my hair with water and squeezed my eyes shut.

Dustin was standing outside the restroom. Jesus, boy, he said. You all right?

Yeah, I mumbled. Just not used to drinking this hard, I guess.

I was going to drive back to the hotel, but Dustin wouldn't hear of it. C'mon, pal, he said. I'll give you a lift. You can pick up your hunk of junk tomorrow.

Dustin swerved through town, running red lights and crashing into curbs. He wouldn't stop talking. I closed my eyes and slept drunkenly.

Eventually we arrived at the hotel. The sun was setting, the sky a bloody tarp thrown over the world, and the leaves were dancing in waltz time. Okay, buddy, Dustin said, shaking my shoulder. Home sweet home. Wake up, Sleeping Beauty.

Somehow I managed to stumble inside the hotel and up the stairs. My stomach was lurching, bile burning my throat. I thought about Lilith and felt good and mad. All I wanted was a lifetime of slumber. I roller-skated down the hallway, the walls swerving from their foundations. I came to my room. My heart gave out. A transplant was years away. Leaning against the wall was a man I'd never seen before. He was tall and wiry with a red slit for a mouth that looked ready to curse. His eyes were gray and his skin was leathery. He wore snakeskin boots, tight slim blue jeans, a jean jacket, and a felt cowboy hat.

He also wore a shiny sheriff's badge.

CHAPTER 7

He took a couple of steps toward me. Mr. Downs? he said with a backcountry drawl.

Yes, sir. It was hard for me to speak. My tongue was bloated and black.

He stuck out a thin hand without a callus visible. Name's Sheriff Baker, he said. I apologize if I startled you. Didn't want to miss you. Night's slow, so I figgered I'd wait for you here. Figgered you'd show up eventually. Figgered right.

I shook his hand. His skin was as soft as a concert pianist. No problem, I said. No problem at all. What do you need? Am I in trouble? I was drinking tonight. Just to pass the time.

No, you ain't in trouble, he said. You ain't in trouble a'tall. Mind if we go into your room? Don't want to wake up all the fine folks that call the Hotel Paisano their home.

We went inside, me first, followed by the Sheriff. He took off his hat and tossed it on the bed. His brown hair was thin and straight, neatly parted to the side. He moved slowly forward, the floorboards creaking under his feet. He pulled back the window curtain and stared down at the street below, his own image twisting in the glass.

He spoke: Wasn't so long ago that this was a respectable little town. Good, honest, God-fearing folks. Folks that were willing to help a stranger just as certain as their own family. Oh, sure, there was the occasional tragedy, but for the most part it was a good town. A safe town. A white town. And now...

All sorts of trash being dumped in our little town. Guess you could say that most of us don't like it one bit. Speakin' of which, how you likin' work at the landfill?

Fine, sir. It's a good job.

He turned around and faced me. Where you from, Mr. Downs?

Ohio originally, I said. But I've been all over. I was on my way to the Mountain when my car broke down. I've liked your little town okay so I decided to stay for a while.

He smiled, but there was no humor in it. You know a fellow named Nick McClellan?

I shook my head. Should I?

He didn't want to answer right away, wanted to make the moment last. You got in a fight with him a few days back. Over at Del's.

I didn't know his name, I said. He was beating on his wife. I told him to cut it out. He didn't take too kindly to my suggestion. So I showed him a thing or two.

Baker grinned. I guess you did. And I don't blame you none. Man shouldn't treat a woman like that, not most of the time anyway. But that fight ain't my concern. Shit, if I investigated every fight in Huerfano County, I'd hardly have time to piss and shit.

So what is your concern?

His eyes met mine and they were hard and mean. Dead hog, he said. Couple days back I got a phone call from Nick. Told me one of his hogs had been butchered. Said somebody slit her throat from end to end. Went down and took a look. Nasty stuff. Ol' Nick was good and pissed. Folks down here don't take too kindly to people destroyin' their livestock. You understand.

I nodded my head because there was nothing else to do. And what does this all have to do with me?

Don't know for sure. When I talked to Nick, he mentioned your name. Mentioned the fight and all. Said he wouldn't be surprised if you was the one. Now I ain't sayin' you did it, but I ain't sayin' you didn't either.

I didn't have anything to do with his hog, I said. Fellow is probably just sore that I whipped him at the bar.

Probably.

Well, I said. Did you want to talk to me about anything else?

He smiled. No, mister, I guess that does it. And you're probably right. Ol' Nick was probably just sore about what happened at the bar.

So then? What do you want from me? I was good and sober now, but my head was throbbing.

Just wanted to have a chat, that's all. Introduce myself, you know.

Pleasure, I said.

We both stood there for a while, and he watched me unblinking.

If there's nothing else, I said, I guess I'll be getting some sleep.

Sure, sure. He took a step forward, stuck out his hand again, and I shook it. When I tried pulling away, he kept on gripping it. He was stronger than I thought. Your truck fixed? he asked.

Yes, sir.

Well, then. You might want to consider movin' along, you know? Just so you don't get into any more trouble.

You ordering me to leave your town?

No, mister. Just a friendly suggestion, that's all.

I pulled my hand from his grip. Have a good evening, Sheriff.

A smile and a wink. You do the same, Joseph.

*   *   *

The days fell in number and everything was wrong. I worked and I drank and I slept. I even paid the hotel whore a few times because I was lonely.

The stranger and the sheriff kept their eyes on me. My brain was bouncing around in my skull.

I didn't see Lilith at all. I thought we were through. It was just as well. I had some cash, the truck was fixed, and the Mountain was waiting. But I couldn't go. I don't know why.

And then one night I was sitting on the hardwood

floor of my hotel room, being drunk, listening to the rain and the radio. The Louvin Brothers, *Satan is Real*.

That's when I heard pounding on the door. I sat there, unable to move. The pounding continued. Unsteadily, I rose to my feet, walked across the room, and pushed open the door. Lilith McClellan stood there, a pathetic heap of a woman.

She was wearing a blue prom-style dress, torn at the shoulder. Her hair was soaking wet, she was shivering, and blood was tricking from her nose. Her cheek was swollen and bruised, her eyes vapid. Oh, Joseph, she whispered, her voice filled with despondency and broken glass.

I pulled her inside, shutting the door behind us. We sat down on the bed and I grabbed a hold of her. What happened? I said. Did your husband do this to you?

She didn't say a word, but the tears began to roll down her battered cheeks, mixing with blood and drugstore mascara.

I'll call the cops, I said. Tell 'em what the old bastard did to you. Then we'll get you to a hospital. I'll drive you there.

No, she said. That's not what I want. I don't want cops. I don't want hospitals.

What are you talking about? You're hurt. Gotta get you taken care of.

She closed her eyes and shook her head. Then she spoke: You once said that it takes courage to kill somebody.

Yes. I believe it does.

So I was wondering. Have you ever killed anybody?

It was all wrong. The mood was pitch-black, and there were strange shadows dancing on the walls. I took a deep breath. I didn't answer right away and when I did, I spoke slowly, cautiously. War changes you, I said. It causes you to do things you didn't think you could do.

Like killing?

Yes. Like killing.

A long pause. Then Lilith reached into her purse and pulled out a pistol. .38 Special. Revolver action.

I eyed the gun dispassionately. Returned my gaze to her face, jaw trembling, nostrils flaring.

She placed the .38 in my hand. My fingers closed around it.

He's a monster, she said.

The world is filled with monsters, I said.

Believe me, I've thought this through. It's the only way. You might think I'm just emotional right now, but I'm not. I know what needs to be done.

And you want me to do it.

Yes. I want you to do it.

I smiled, shook my head. I'm not killing anybody, I said. My voice sounded strange, out of place. I'll take you away with me, but I'm not killing anybody.

He's got a life insurance plan, she said. It's good money. More than we could ever earn.

I grinned thin-lipped. So that's what this is about? Money?

She wiped away a crimson tear. It's about a lot of things. But the money would help, don't you think? I mean, let's be real, how much do you have? Not enough for us to live on, I bet.

I didn't answer, just stared at the pistol in my

hand. My brain was soaking in kerosene. A strike of a match and…

Somberly, I placed the weapon on the windowsill. Then I turned back around and spoke, my voice quiet, measured. Let's talk about something else, I said.

What…what do you want to talk about?

Let's talk about your other boyfriend. I saw you at the bar the other day. I saw you with that Mexican. The two of you were having a hell of a time.

She rose from the bed, her parted lips coated with blood. Oh, Joseph, she said. That guy, he—

Means nothing to you, right? Is that what you were going to say?

I've known him for a while. We get together now and then. That night, well I was drunk. I was lonely. You weren't around. I'm sorry, Joseph, I'm so sorry. I know I'm a whore. I've always been a whore. But it doesn't change the fact that I love you. It doesn't change the fact that I want to be with you.

It was funny, what she said, so I laughed. I laughed and laughed and hiccupped and laughed. I just couldn't stop. A minute or more without pause. Lilith begged me to stop. I only laughed some more.

I…I don't know what else you want me to say, she said. All I can do is say that I'm sorry and that I love you and—

My laughter ceased but my grin remained. You don't need to apologize, I said. You only have to do one thing for me. Just one thing.

What is it? I'll do anything for you, Joseph, you know that.

Just keep lying to me. That's all I need. That's all I've ever needed.

Corrosion

I picked up the gun and aimed it at her head. Instinctively, she covered her face with her hands. But I didn't shoot. I didn't want to hurt her. She was a broken angel and I loved her. I said: I'll do it. I'll shoot him in the skull and then we'll be together for a spell. You just keep on lying and I'll keep on lying and we'll be happier than hell.

CHAPTER 8

The next morning, I sat on the windowsill and stared down at the street below.

An old man with overalls and a washed-out face stood on the curb reading a newspaper. A couple of high school kids sat on the hood of a truck; he was pulling her close and she was resting her head on his shoulder. A woman wearing a long flower dress and carrying a grocery bag in either arm trudged down the sidewalk, a ragamuffin little girl following a few steps behind. And there was the whore from the hotel, her face wind-chapped and spiteful...

Outside, the wind was picking up, and I could hear some trash cans crashing against the asphalt like drunks on a dance floor. I pulled out my can of snuff and snorted a pinch. Then I squeezed my eyes shut, tried to sleep. That's when the vision came to me. A memory or a premonition. A vision so vivid that I started twitching and jerking, fingers covering my mouth in terror.

I'm on the Mountain and the snow is falling. I'm just standing there, a homemade axe slung over my shoulder, gazing at the old shack, wood rotting before my eyes. And then I look up and see a figure, monstrous and translucent, dart from behind a collapsed mine and vanish into the trees. Trancelike, I move away from the shack and start toward the thick forest where the creature has vanished. Dead branches and dead leaves crunch beneath my feet, the winter snow whitening the high hills of hell.

Within the woods, ancient and deep, the pines sway back and forth in unison, the shadows swarming and lunging. The sun peaks through the clouds and reflects brightly against the dirty snow. I swivel my head, searching for the strange creature. Nothing but trees and snow and frozen weeds. I look down. I see footprints, barely visible. Eyes peeled on the ground, I follow the footsteps as they wind through the mountain trees. I quicken my pace. My breathing is heavy and irregular. Off to the right, a stream flows gently, blanketed by snow. Somewhere an eagle screams.

I walk a long ways, far away from the mining shack. Then the footsteps are gone and so is my shadow. I tromp through drifts of calf-deep snow, breathing hard. I catch another glimpse of the stream, dark under snow and ice and branches.

And then I see the opening of a cavern. The sun is sinking behind the jagged peaks, and the sky is a muted pink. Several large stones block the cave's opening. I get to my knees, drop my axe to the ground. The stones are lodged into the dirt, made heavy by the snow. It takes me some time to pull them away and when I look at my fingers, I see that they are bleeding.

Jon Bassoff

On my hands and knees, dragging the axe behind me, I enter the cave. Everything is dark, the light vanishing completely as soon as I pass the first bend. Reaching into my pocket, I pull out a lighter and strike it on. The rocks are pale and seem ready to collapse inward at any moment. The dirt floor is damp. It smells of a primeval pool of water, of mildew and rot.

Then the lighter goes out. I strike it a few times but it doesn't take. I toss it aside and continue onward, unable to see my hand an inch in front of my face. From somewhere outside the cave I hear what sounds like shouting, a ghostly Comanche battle cry. And then another sound: an echo of high-pitched shrieks followed by a thunderous whooshing and then my own screams as a colony of invisible bats fly around my head, hungry for feeding time.

I continue crawling through the tunnel as it becomes narrower and narrower. And then the sudden onset of light. I tilt my head upward. There is an opening in the ceiling, not much more than a foot in diameter, and the final remains of light filter through.

Just ahead, the walls widen into an underground room, the end of the passageway. I straighten up and step inside. My fingers are bleeding badly and I'm shivering. I can see the plumes of my breath.

On the dirt floor are several cans, all opened and emptied. Beans and corn and soup and apple juice. Smashed and rusted. There is a wool blanket, all tattered and torn and eaten through. And lying on the blanket, what looks to be the remains of an old lurid graphic novel. I bend down and pick it up. It is waterlogged and nearly disintegrates in my hands, but I can still make out the artwork on the cover: a muscular and heavily tattooed soldier brandishing a machine gun, about to shoot through the skull of a knife-

wielding, turban-wearing Arab. Fight to the Finish *it's called. I drop the comic to the ground and stare up at the wall. Black scrawl written in the handwriting of a child: I am because I am because I am because I am.*

And then he appears. A boy of about sixteen. Face sickly, eyes wild. He wears a wide-brimmed preacher's hat. He takes a few steps forward. I know who you are, he says. I raise my axe. He's unconcerned. He continues walking toward me. I know who you are, he says again. When he's no more than a step away from me, he covers his face with his hat. I can hardly breathe. A moment later he removes the hat and I can see that his face is melting, skin dripping to the cavern floor like wax. I drop my axe to the ground and he's laughing and laughing and I realize that I'm staring at my own face…

*   *   *

Two days later, three in the morning, wind blowing hard. Lilith was gone. We'd made some plans before she'd left. They weren't all that well thought out. I'm gonna be staying with my aunt in Rifle, she'd said. I'll stay there for two nights. Here's the key. You might have to jiggle it a bit. And walk lightly. The floor creaks. It shouldn't matter. He's a sound sleeper. Especially when he drinks. He always drinks.

It didn't get any lonelier than this. I put on my jacket. I walked down the hallway of the hotel. One of the room doors opened and a man stood there with thick yellow-gray hair, slicked back into a pompadour. His cheeks were ruddy, his eyes cloudy. His hands were covered with lesions. He wore a too-small white T-shirt, his belly bulging out the bottom.

I nodded at him. He watched me walk down the hall, and then I heard the door close.

I didn't want anybody else to see me, so I climbed down the fire escape, tearing the cuff on my jeans. I leapt to the ground and landed awkwardly, rolling onto my side. I got to my feet and wiped myself off. I pulled up the collar of my camouflage jacket and stuck my hands in my pockets. Then I got in my truck and hit the engine.

Outside, the sky was black and the moon was a sliver of china. I felt more than a little tense. I kept worrying that I was being followed by the stranger or the sheriff, kept glancing in the rearview mirror, but there was nothing but gnarled junipers and cottonwoods.

The radio was playing static and my skull was filling with blood. I searched for some pleasant memories. Carving pumpkins with my mother at the kitchen table while the autumn leaves fall lazily to the ground. Sledding down a steep hill, the snowflakes landing on my tongue. Tossing a baseball with my father, knowing smiles on our faces as the ball smacks against the leather. Sitting by the lake on a lazy summer afternoon, watching the tadpoles dart through the water. But these times had never happened, and they were soon replaced by a more grotesque image: a woman lying on a canopy bed, maggots crawling in her eye sockets, a wooden cross hanging upside down on the wall. I squeezed my eyes shut, drove blindly.

At the McClellan house. Sitting in the ghost truck, breathing deeply, staring at the darkened windows. Knowing that fate was relentless. No sense in fighting. I pushed open the door, stepped outside. Sweat dribbled down my face. Everything was silent except for an owl hooting. I walked slowly, the gravel crunching beneath my boots.

The lights were out and the pigs were sleeping. I stood at the front door. A tin can blew across the porch. It startled me. I opened the screen door. I pulled out the key from my shirt pocket. The wind was blowing and my hands were trembling. It took me thirty seconds or more to get the key in the lock. Slowly, I turned the key and pulled it out. I twisted the handle and pushed open the door.

I stepped inside. It was pitch-black. I pulled out my penlight and turned it on. I walked through the living room, my boots echoing softly on the hardwood floor. Strange shadows filled the room. It was hard not to feel disoriented. I walked down the hallway, slowly, uncertainly. The floor wouldn't stop creaking. I thought I heard something else, a low grinding sound. I noticed that I wasn't breathing...

The door to their bedroom was slightly ajar. I opened it slowly. The curtains were open and the moonlight was shining through. I turned off my penlight, placed it in my pocket. Nick's clothes were crumpled on the floor and his boots were resting by his bed. He was lying on top of the blanket, arms at his side, stomach rising and falling gently. I stood in the doorway, watching, watching.

The silence of the house was getting to be too much and I was filled with anxiety. I walked cautiously toward the slumbering figure and the oak floorboards creaked again. I paused. My heart was pounding in my rib cage and my head was throbbing. I took a few more steps forward. The gun dangled from my hand. Nick stirred, sighing deeply, shifting his arm to shield his eyes. I stood there, not moving, not blinking.

There was a pillow at the foot of the bed. I picked it up, my fingers digging into the stuffing. For a moment I thought about turning around, walking right out that door. Then I thought of Lilith and everything slipped my mind. I sucked in a giant breath and then I pounced. I smothered his face with the pillow and he jerked awake, flailing like a cutthroat trout. I jammed the gun where I figured his mouth to be and fired once, twice, three times. His body jerked a few times, then it relaxed, arms falling back to his side, head lolling onto his shoulder.

I pulled away the pillow and dropped it on the bed. His face was a bloody mess, his eyes opened wide. Nick McClellan was more than a little bit dead.

CHAPTER 9

I felt like I was going to be sick. I stuffed the gun in the front of my pants and backed away. The room was spinning *Wizard of Oz* style. A crate of chickens and two men in a rowboat flew outside the window.

I staggered through the house, wiping down doorknobs and every trace of my presence. I kicked open the front door and let it slam shut behind me. I glanced around. No sign of life anywhere. A man was dead and nobody knew. So what? People die every second. The snow had started falling, the mean old wind blowing it every which way. I shoved my hands in my pockets and quickened my pace. My body was getting cold. I couldn't stop shivering.

The black shadows of the Rocky Mountains loomed up ahead. There were no sounds but my heart beating and the wind through the windmills and skeleton trees. With the gun in my pocket, I pulled up the collar of my jacket and made my way hurriedly back toward the pickup. The snow had accumulated enough that I was leaving tracks. I'd have to throw my boots away just as soon as I got back to the hotel...

I thought about the whole situation, and I felt a little bit queasy. A man dies and there's no turning back. It's finished, and that means for always. But none of it mattered. We've all got to die sometime. And Nick McClellan had all but begged for it. The way he'd treated Lilith. I'd seen the bruises. I'd seen the blood. A man like that...he didn't deserve to live any more than a rabid dog. So why couldn't I shake this uneasy feeling?

I drove, my hands gripping the wheel tightly. The radio was tuned to a fascist talk show, the words a blur of hatred. Snow blew into the windshield, making it hard to see. My breathing was slow and labored.

Nothing but a socialist and a Marxist and a Muslim, the man shouted. My mind was filled with static. And then rising above the static, the sound of a siren, muted and ghostly. I glanced in the rearview mirror and saw red, yellow, and blue lights flashing, tearing the night in half.

I didn't slow down, not right away. The gun lay on the seat next to me, lonely and menacing. Resigned to my fate, I hit the brakes, pulled over to the side of the road. But the trooper didn't stop and my truck shook as he sped past. I stayed on the side of the road for a while, hands shaking, shoulders heaving. And then I felt like maybe the Lord Jesus was looking out for me, and my body relaxed some. I thought about Lilith, thought about her milk-white skin, her heart-shaped lips, and for a moment, just a moment, thought that salvation was in reach…

*   *   *

About two miles west of the McClellan household there was an abandoned grange. And behind the farmhouse, leaning forward like a drunk ready to vomit, a dried-up water well, the metal bucket still hanging from a rope. I got out of the car, grabbed the killing weapon, and walked toward the well, snow crunching beneath my feet, breath pluming from my mouth. I stood over the well and looked down into a black abyss. Clenching my jaw, I placed the gun over the edge of the well. Then I released my grip and the weapon fell, splashing into the dank water.

*   *   *

Fifteen minutes later, I was back at the hotel. The sky had lightened to a bubblegum pink, but nearly all the rooms were still dark. I walked through the hotel lobby and I kept thinking that I saw a figure skulking at the perimeter of the room. I made my way up the staircase and there were dead-man shadows on the wall. I continued down the hallway, stepping over warped floorboards and olden moans, and came to my room and shoved open the door. The window was open a crack and the room was cold. I pushed down the window, then quickly stripped out of my clothes and dropped them on the rusted radiator.

For a long time, I sat huddling in the bed, shivering, pretty sure that all hell was about to break loose.

*   *   *

The next couple of days weren't much of anything. Mostly I just sat in my hotel room and chewed tobacco and drank brandy. It was okay. Nobody bothered me. I tried calling Lilith a few times but she didn't answer. It was just as well.

Sometimes I'd go into town, walk around a bit. I kept my eyes open for the stranger, kept my eyes open for the sheriff. I didn't see either one of them, but I felt their presence, yes I did. I read through the local paper, watched the evening news. There was no mention of any murder...

Dustin called me on the phone. Where the hell are you? he said. Your shift started an hour ago. The boss man ain't pleased.

Tell him I quit, I said.

Now come on, Joseph. Jobs ain't easy to come by these days. I can make up an excuse for you. Say you've got diarrhea or some shit. No need to be rash, my friend.

Things have changed. I don't need a job no more.

You win the lottery?

No lottery. Change of priorities, is all.

Yeah?

You make the realization that we don't ride the train, the train rides us.

What the hell are you talking about?

I'll be seeing you, Dustin.

*   *   *

71

Corrosion

My hotel room was beginning to smell. Something was dead. A rat maybe. Smell triggers memories…

Remember that woman? Nothing but skin and bones inside a long white nightgown. Body covered with sores oozing blue fibers, white threads, and little black specks…

Remember that old man? Gnashing his teeth and tearing his clothes. Wailing in the small hours of the night. Praying on scabbed knees…

Remember that boy? Sitting on the end of the bed watching her. Tiptoeing through the hallways, the soundtrack of organ music echoing against the walls, the language of God splattering on the linoleum…

Remember those neighbors? Knocking on the door, making all kinds of inquiries. Showing up at night spraying Lysol around the base of the house…

*   *   *

Eventually, I got a hold of Lilith. She didn't sound like herself. Who is this? she said.

You know who this is, I said, my voice raspy and crackling.

Lilith didn't speak. I could hear her breathing.

It's all done, I said. He won't be bothering you no more, no how.

More silence.

He begged for mercy. Some people don't deserve mercy.

Jesus, she said, voice trembling. You're serious.

Hell yes, I'm serious. When can I see you? I need to see you.

I don't know. Fuck. Don't call me anymore.

Jon Bassoff

What?

It's over, Joseph. Don't you see?

Wait a second. I—

The phone clicked dead. I slammed the receiver down, and the phone exploded, the chassis and circuit board landing across the room.

I lay on my bed and stared at the ceiling. I rubbed my temple with my thumb. Terrible images appeared behind my eyes. A little Iraqi girl leaning against a smoldering building, staring at me with those big brown eyes...An American soldier, his bare arms bronzed and buff, tossing a baby in the air and impaling it on his Civil War bayonet...Walking through a deep and loathsome valley, pulled along by a faceless man, a river of blood boiling down below...Gazing into an endless pit, malformed bodies writhing against one another, scratching away their diseased skin...

This world was getting to be too much.

CHAPTER 10

He wore a mask. A white rubber mask pulled across his face as tightly as a drumhead, tufts of iron-gray hair sprouting wildly from beneath his wide-brimmed black hat. And behind the mask, nothing but black holes for eyes, like those of dead man. He stood on a wooden crate outside of Del's Lounge bellowing out in a booming voice. He wore a string tie and torn frock coat and waved around a tattered Bible high in the air, preaching about Satan and Salvation, about Heaven and Hell, about Sin, Sin, Sin.

Shouting: And God shall cast wicked men into hell at any moment! His shovel is in his hand, and he will gather his wheat into the garner and then he will burn up the chaff with unquenchable fire! Yes, justice calls for the evildoers to be thus cast into hell and makes no objection against God's destruction. And hear me when I say that every nonbeliever belongs to hell; that is his place!

Yes, brothers, yes, sisters, I have been to dozens of towns all across this country, from ocean to ocean, from desert floor to mountain top, and never before have I been in a town that reeks so much of sin! Boozing and whoring, stealing and raping! You are truly the people of Gomorrah and you shall be consumed by fire and brimstone! But perhaps it is not too late. Now is the time to awaken to the deafening calls of God's word and fly from the wrath to come. Sinners, sinners: escape for your lives, look not behind you, escape from this world, lest you be consumed!

And a few people stopped and listened, and a few people laughed or shouted obscenities. But this merchant of the damned kept right on preaching, his wrath not concealed by the rubber mask. Shouting: All of you sinners who have not accepted the word of Jesus Christ, you're fooling yourself! You're in denial of the grandest kind! And this denial will lead you to feeling the burning horrors of hell, where the worm dieth not, and the fire is never quenched! Hell: a place of awful torment. Hell: a place where unconverted men spend an endless eternity, without hope. Yes, you unconverted sinners, soon you'll be dead and you'll learn all about what you have lost!

One pear-shaped woman wearing an oversized parka tried giving him money, and the masked prophet became incensed, shouting, I ain't no televangelist! I ain't no B-grade grifter! I'm a prophet for almighty Jesus, and my payment will come in the afterworld! And the woman picked up that one-dollar bill and stuffed it into her coat pocket, hurrying away with an anxious smile on her face.

As for me, I couldn't stop watching him because

Corrosion

I knew him so well, from another life. And he didn't notice me, hidden in the shadows...

And then the door to the bar opened and a group of people exited—four or five roughnecks and a whore of a woman. They were all were drunk and spoke in voices loud and cruel.

The masked prophet saw his opportunity. He grabbed one of them by the arm and, with a voice full of fervor, said: Jesus saved me, yes he did. He dragged me from the river of swine and gave me life that I didn't deserve. And in return I made a promise to him. I promised that I would go from town to town and tell the truth to every last one of you. And here's the truth: A life without Jesus ain't no life at all. A life without Jesus is a life with the devil. A life without Jesus means eternal damnation. And hell is hotter than a blast furnace! He paused for a moment and pointed both fingers at his mask. People wonder about the mask. People say, Reverend Wells, why do you hide? That mask scares us. Show us your face. But I don't dare! You see, it would be too shocking for the likes of you. Your eyes would bug out of your skull, and the bile would coat your throat. Because beneath this here mask is a face of heartache! Beneath this here mask is a face of sin! Let this be a warning to you. You stay on your present path, and this is what your soul will look like. And no mask can hide a hell-bound soul!

Then the reverend raised his arms like Christ in Rio de Janeiro. Mustering all the power he could in his devil's voice, he glared at the roughnecks and the whore and said: Oh, yes, I know a thing or two about sin! Drinking, whoring, fighting. I am here to tell you that I was a marionette with the devil as his puppeteer. My toes could feel the heat of hell getting closer and closer. But then I had a vision! A vision of God himself! You laugh! You say I'm crazy! But I tell you the truth. God Almighty spoke to me! And here's what he told me: He told me to go to Hal's Hardware down there in El Hornillo, Texas, and buy myself a bottle of lye. And I didn't ask questions! Like Abraham, ready to sacrifice his only son, I did what I was told. And I sat inside a worn-out motel room and waited for my next instructions. Days passed until I heard from him again. The temperature must have been 110 degrees and the sweat was pouring down my face. And when he whispered in my ear, I was weak with dehydration. But what I heard wasn't no aural hallucination. The Good Lord told me to open up that bottle of lye and douse my handsome face completely and absolutely. Straight from the Lord's mouth! And I followed his word on that day, and I've followed his word every day since! Can't you understand? I burned my face, so I wouldn't have to burn my soul!

And as the people gasped and murmured, he kept right on talking, fists clenched tightly. And now I ask you to take a look at yourselves. Can you do it? You're nothing but whores, thieves, and liars! You think you can hide from your destiny? It's just a matter of time. You'll try to huddle beneath the Lord's cloak, but it won't do you no good. The Good Lord is ready to burn the chaff!

I could listen to this filth no longer. I stepped out from beneath the shadows and showed my own face of heartache, my own face of sin. I said: Is this the face you're preaching about? And the crowd was silent and so was Reverend Wells.

My hands were suddenly clenched into fists. I stepped up to the reverend, shouted: You don't know me! My face may be hideous, but my soul is pure! What gives you the right?

A face of sin! he shouted.

No sir, I said. A face of war!

As I figured! A murderer by any other name! How many did you kill, young man? How many casualties of war? How many sins must be negotiated in the afterlife?

I'd heard enough. With adrenaline flowing, I stepped up and gave the masked prophet a quick punch to his chest. The suddenness of my movement caught him by surprise, and he lost his balance. He started wobbling like a barroom drunk, grabbing at the air for support. Filled with rage, I took two quick steps and pile-drove him into the ground. Then I reached back and slammed my fist into his masked face, once, twice, three times. He'd feel some pain now. I really let him have it. Blows to the face, to the body, to the back of the head.

Meanwhile, the whore of a woman was screaming and moaning, and a couple of the drunkards were trying to pull me off the preacher, who was lying on the ground shielding his invisible face with his arm. I yanked at the mask and he suddenly came to life, kicking and screaming. After a long struggle, I managed to pull the rubber mask off his head completely.

His face wasn't burned at all. No, his skin was smooth and healthy, and I knew he was no prophet. A phony! I shouted. A goddamn phony! With renewed fury, I slammed his face with my fist, over and over and over again, tearing up his skin, creating a bloody mess.

Eventually a couple of the men managed to drag me off the conman and pin me to the ground. Phony! I kept shouting. Soon I heard the ambient of a siren. I watched, still good and enraged, as a big sheriff's SUV pulled up at the curb and Sheriff Baker stepped out. He adjusted his Stetson hat, blew on his hands, and started walking slowly, wearily to the chaotic scene. He nodded at the bearded drunks twisting back my arms, and said: All right boys, let 'im go.

CHAPTER 11

The drunks released my arms, pushed me to the ground. The false prophet sat up, touching his torn face in horror, mumbling about the fiery furnaces. Baker looked me up and down and shook his head. Now lookie here, he said. If it ain't Stratton's public enemy number one. What kind of trouble have you gotten into this time?

I was minding my own business, I said. It's the preacher you should worry about.

Baker grinned before reading me my rights. Then the deputy sheriff, a brutish-looking fellow with a snaggletooth, handcuffed me, pushed my head down, and shoved me into the backseat of the patrol car. My fingers were aching, bones crushed for sure.

We drove around for a while, the lawmen speaking in hushed whispers, before ending at the local jail, a decaying old brick building a couple miles east of town. Once inside, they fingerprinted me and took my mug shot. Then they strip-searched me. They confiscated my wallet, a book of matches, my snuff, and a deck of cards with naked women on the back. My belongings were placed into an envelope, and the recording officer gave me a receipt. I was given the option of a phone call. Nobody wanted to hear from me.

They tossed me into a small holding cell with a few dirty Mexicans and a couple of tattooed rednecks. One of the rednecks looked me over and shook his head. I wasn't good enough even for his tastes.

*   *   *

The next day they cuffed my hands behind my back and escorted me down the hallway to another cell. The burlier of the guards shoved me inside, and the other one locked the metal door. Without a word they turned and walked away, their footsteps echoing in unison.

The cell was stark. A mattress, a toilet, a sink. A small window covered with bars. Obscene messages written on the concrete walls. I lay on the mattress and folded my hands behind my head. Off in the distance I could hear the screams of the inmates echoing throughout the concrete hallway. I squeezed my eyes tight and covered my ears with my hands. Soon I was asleep. I dreamed about urban warfare—buildings turned to rubble, children charred beyond recognition.

When I awoke, the screaming had stopped and everything was dark. I began to panic. I wasn't afraid of the dark, but I was afraid of what might happen in the dark. I shook the bars and shouted for a guard. Nobody came. Terrified, I huddled in the corner of the cell, the smell of blood and urine rising in my nostrils.

*   *   *

All the next day I paced back in forth in my cage, the fluorescent lights flickering and the steel doors echoing throughout the corridor. Every so often a group of men wearing identical blue suits and red ties appeared outside my cell, talking in hushed tones behind hands. I shouted at them, asked about my arraignment, asked about legal representation, but they only shook their heads and jotted down notes in spiral notebooks.

And then, later on, while I was lying on the cement floor listening to my own dire thoughts ricocheting through my skull, I heard the jangle of keys and watched as the door banged open and a pair of guards entered with hands on their guns. And directly behind them, Sheriff Baker, Stetson hat perched on his head. With a slight nod, and something approaching a smile, he took a few steps until he was standing directly over me.

How ya doin, Joseph? he said.

I sat up and glared at Baker's wind-chapped face. Why am I still here? I said. Why haven't I had an arraignment? Why haven't I been assigned a lawyer?

You'll get your lawyer, he said. You'll get your arraignment.

He nodded toward the guards and they exited the

cell, staying within earshot down the corridor, arms folded on chests.

Baker pulled out a can of Rooster, snapping his wrist a few times to pack it. He offered me a dip and I shook my head. He took an oversized pinch and stuck it between his lower lip and gum. Then he grinned with black-speckled teeth.

He leaned up against the wall and shook his head and the grin slowly faded away. I been doin' this job a long time, he said. Usually it's a pretty quiet town, Stratton is. Some domestic violence here and there, maybe a drunken brawl or two, but nothin' like this. He leaned over the toilet and spat a thick brown dollop.

You talking about the preacher? I said. Or are you still fretting about the pig?

He glared at me for a long moment. Then he wiped his mouth with the back of his hand and shook his head. We ain't worried about the pig no more. And we ain't too concerned about that phony preacher.

Well then?

Baker removed his hat and placed it on the bed. Then he sat down. I was still sitting on the floor. From somewhere down the corridor a prisoner shrieked, the sound reverberating against the walls and floors.

Didn't you know you'd be our first suspect? Baker asked, his voice a low growl.

What are you talking about?

You know what I'm talkin' about. Your buddy. Nick McClellan. He was shot dead while he slept. Three bullets. Through a down pillow.

I was caught off guard, rusty nails jammed in my gut. I kept it together, shook my head. Said: I don't know a thing about it.

He was found yesterday evening by his wife. You remember his wife don't you? Sexy little number? Sometimes a redhead, sometimes not?

I didn't kill that man, I said. How could I have? I was locked in here.

They placed the time of death a full 48 hours before you got into your little philosophical fight. Sometime after midnight the night before last. You weren't in jail that night. Wanna try again?

Sure, I said. I was in the Paisano that night. You can ask the owner. She saw me. I didn't leave my room all night.

That's the best you can do?

It's the truth.

We've got a witness. Saw you leaving your room early in the morning. Face like yours, kinda hard to miss.

I didn't kill that man, I said again.

No. Sure you didn't. Let me ask you a question, though. How long you been screwing his wife?

Fuck you.

Damn it, Downs. We had a little talk with Lilith. She told us a few things. How you bloodied up Nick after he'd gotten rough with her. How she followed you to the Paisano. How she showed you her grati- tude. How she kept coming back.

Doesn't mean anything, I said.

She told us how you fell hard for her. How you started talking crazy. Talking about offing the old man. Talking about life insurance money and a new start in the hills. She didn't take you seriously. But when she found her husband's body, she changed her mind a bit.

Something like rage spread through my body. Not at being accused of murder. Rage at knowing I'd been betrayed. Rage at knowing she'd been unfaithful. Rage at knowing she was just like all the others...

I rose to my feet and walked to the steel door. I gripped the bars tightly and hung my head. I pictured Lilith's face and my hands around her throat...

Over the next hour, Baker asked the same questions, over and over again. Only they were phrased in different ways. He played nice: You were just trying to protect her, he said. You gave him what he deserved. He played mean: Gotta talk, Joseph, or the state will kill you for sure!

I knew his games. I knew his motivations. I didn't break. I asked for a lawyer. He pretended not to hear. I was at the precipice of sanity...

CHAPTER 12

He finally ceased the interrogations, allowed me to sleep. Still, it was no good. The world was filled with moaning and laughing and metal doors slamming. Walls and pipes ringing in a secret code. I covered my ears with my hands. I squeezed my eyes tight. A tooth in my mouth was aching, rotting by the minute. I yanked at it with my fingers.

 I thought about Lilith, about the tattoo on her breast. I thought about what I might do to her if I ever got out of this place.

I must have slept a little bit because I was jarred awake by a guard pounding on my cage with his billy club, shouting out my last name. I opened my eyes. It took a moment for them to adjust. The guard was a big man with a bald white head and a belly bulging over his belt. They all had murderers' eyes, these guards.

Jon Bassoff

Rise and shine, he said. The judge is ready for you.

He entered my cell and snapped on leg irons and handcuffs, then led me out of the cell into the corridor where the caged felons shouted and whistled and shook the bars. And along the way we picked up another half-dozen prisoners, their eyes beady and mean. But nobody gave me any lip, nobody at all, because my face was grotesque and even the devil can be frightened.

We were led outside and loaded onto a black-and-white bus with the words *Huerfano County Prison* on the side. There was a guard behind us and a guard in front of us and they both carried rifles and were ready to use them. We sat down in the bus and were told to keep our goddamn mouths shut, and it was just like a field trip, except we were going to the courthouse to get our charges read.

It was a twenty-minute drive. Nobody spoke. The courthouse stood in the shadows of a giant grain elevator. It was a menacing old concrete building that looked to have been converted from a hospital of some kind. We were led into the backside of the building and into another holding cell. This one here not much different from the one in the jail, except smaller and danker.

After a short wait, we were summoned, and the deputies marched us into a tiny courtroom two at a time. It was there that a plump old man with a rumpled suit, raggedly sheered hair, and oversized glasses approached me and patted me on the shoulder. Name's Desmond Harris, he said. I'll be representing you, understand? Try my best to get you out on bail,

87

understand?

Bail?

You're a war hero. You're not a threat to society. You're the savior of society. Get you out on bail, hear me?

The judge looked like all judges do. Balding gray hair. Glasses resting on the tip of his nose. An expression of sternness or smugness. He called my name and Mr. Harris grabbed my arm and led me in front of the judge. The judge spent a few moments studying my file. He looked at me over his glasses, his lips curled into a frown.

Mr. Downs, he said. Are you aware of the charges brought against you?

I nodded my head and said I was.

You don't need to make a plea at this time.

I understand.

Your preliminary hearing is scheduled for Monday, December 2nd.

At that moment, my lawyer put up his finger. Your Honor, he said. We move to have my client free on bail. He does not have any prior offenses, not even a traffic ticket. He is veteran of the Iraq war. He served with distinction.

A soldier, huh?

I nodded my head. Yes, sir. 1st Battalion, 7th Regiment, 1st Division. Stationed in Mosul.

The judge watched me for a few moments and then nodded his head slowly. We owe you a debt of gratitude, he said.

Thank you, sir.

I hope you didn't do the things they said you done.

No, sir. I didn't.

Under the circumstances, the judge said, considering the lack of priors and valor in which he served, bail is set for $750,000. He slammed the gavel down. Next case.

The other lawyer, a slick-looking fellow with bright white teeth and a bright red tie, didn't like this resolution. Your Honor, he said. I think you should reconsider. He's charged with first-degree murder.

The judge took off his glasses and glared at the shyster. Only charged, he said. I've made my decision. $750,000.

My lawyer said something to me that I didn't understand. I was supposed to be thankful. $750,000? That meant, what $75,000 to a bail bondsman? It was as good as no bail. The sheriff's deputies marched me back to the courthouse holding area. It wouldn't be long now. They'd delouse me, wash me down, issue me a jail uniform, a towel, a bedroll, and then lead me back to that steel cage...

*   *   *

The next few nights, I died a million deaths. Hanging from a gnarled branch of a chestnut tree. Submerging slowly into a scum-covered pond. Bleeding profusely from jagged wounds on my wrists...

Then early the next morning, as I lay on my cot staring at the cracks in the cement ceiling, a long shadow spread across my cell. I could hear those keys jangling again, then the *thwunk* of the steel door opening. I sat up. A barrel-chested, baby-faced guard stood in the doorway gripping his billy club tightly.

Joseph Downs? he said.

I rose to my feet. Yes, sir.

Come with me.

He grabbed me by the arm and we walked through the corridor. Where are we going? I said.

You've been bailed out, he said.

Bailed out?

Yes, sir.

Who bailed me out?

He didn't answer.

We reached the front desk. The cop behind the desk asked me to sign a paper before pulling out a bag with my clothes and belongings. He gave me another paper, which had the date of my next court appearance. And that was it. I was free to go. I reached into the bag and pulled out my snuff, stuck a pinch in my mouth. Then I nodded at the officer. Be seeing you around, I said. And I left.

*   *   *

I didn't know what to make of all this. I didn't have a friend in the world. Outside the air was cold and the wind was howling.

I walked down the highway, sticking out my thumb. Every now and then a car would slow down, but when they caught a look at my face, they sped right on up. I buried my hands in my pocket, mumbled a prayer to God.

When I finally arrived back at the Hotel Paisano, the moon was being smothered by a blanket of clouds. I snuck in the back door and walked up the stairs. Somewhere a phone was ringing, never picked up, lonely, lonely, lonely. I finally got to my door, shoved it open. It had been days. My suitcase was gone. And that's not all. A skinny old man with a concave chest and Einstein hair was sitting on the bed, his eyes rolled straight back in his head. The town whore was sitting on her knees, humming an American tune. Her wig was pink and her back was bare. I watched for a moment. Then I shut the door.

I sat in the hallway and played mumblety peg with my knife. And I got to thinking about how it sure was lucky that I'd gotten out of the war alive, and it sure was lucky that I'd been bailed out of jail, and it sure was sure that one of these days I'd pay Lilith McClellan a visit...

I went down to the lobby. The blue-haired woman was behind the desk, head resting on the counter. I pounded on the counter a few times and she jerked awake. When she saw my face, she released a muffled scream. It took her a moment to compose herself.

I'm sorry, she said. You startled me.

My room, I said. I wasn't done with it.

I assumed you would be gone for some time...

Where's my suitcase?

She nodded toward a closet. I'll get it for you, she said. Miscommunication is all. I hope you return to the Hotel Paisano next time you're passing through...

*   *   *

I stayed in my car that night. I snorted snuff, drank brandy, listened to The Handsome Family. At some point it started to rain and it was a lullaby and I drifted to sleep.

Corrosion

I dreamed of Lilith and we were dancing in that old miner's cabin and calliope music was playing and the floor was covered with rats, several layers deep, crawling over each other, gnawing on rodent corpses and I pulled Lilith close and her skin was missing, there was just a bleach-white skull, and I was walking down a darkened stairway...

*   *   *

I awoke to the sound of tapping on the window. My heart ruptured and my eyes flew open. With trepidation, I rolled down the window. A flashlight shone into my face. I squinted and shielded my eyes with my arm. The wind was howling and the rain was falling slantways. Winter trudging forward. The flashlight lowered and I saw cruel eyes under a gray wool hat. The stranger. I opened my mouth, ready to say something.

He raised a 12-gauge pump-action shotgun and aimed it at my forehead.

CHAPTER 13

Unlock the door, he said, motioning toward the passenger's side. I pulled up the lock. The stranger walked around the back of the car, his shotgun still pointed at my poor head. He yanked open the door and sat inside. His eyes were all bloodshot and he smelled like Petron.

Start the car, he said. We're going for a drive.

And so we drove. He guided my driving, told me how fast to go, when to turn, all the while keeping the weapon straight and steady.

Eventually we made our way onto Highway 52. It was a good deal past midnight; there were no other cars on the road. I could hear him breathing, wheezing. I wondered if he was going to shoot me. I wondered if I'd see my body from above. Another couple of miles, he said.

I didn't ask him any questions. I didn't ask who he was. I didn't ask what he wanted. He'd tell me soon. Or he wouldn't. It didn't really matter. None of it really mattered…

There was a sign for a town called Dacono. He told me to exit. The snow was falling harder now and it was hard to see. I turned on my brights, but it only made it worse. We drove down a county line road, surrounded by whitened wheat fields, before passing through a little town with nothing but a farmer bar and a post office. We turned onto a little dirt road and drove for a while. Then he told me to stop.

We were at the end of the world and this man here was the devil and he was waiting for payment…

Turn off the engine, he said.

I did as I was told.

Did you kill that man, Nick McClellan?

I didn't answer.

You can tell me. It won't make a difference now. Besides. Don't you think I deserve to know? After emptying my savings to bail you out?

I turned and faced him. My mouth was dry. My head was spinning. It wasn't going to be long now.

What do you want from me? I whispered.

He didn't answer for a moment. Then he took the shotgun and slammed the barrel against my temple. My head smashed into the window. I covered my face with my hands. He aimed the pump-action gun at my face. You know what's gonna happen, Private? he shouted. Your skull's gonna crack like a coconut!

After that he didn't say anything for a long while. Eventually his hands tired, and he lowered the weapon, placed it on his lap. I eyed it cautiously, thought about making a move. Thought better of it. Through the brooding gloom, his cheeks appeared sunken, his skin yellow. When he did speak again, his voice was filled with tempests, disease, and death. He said: Let me tell you about my son. There's some things you should know.

And suddenly, I knew where this was headed and I didn't want to hear.

A soldier. Like you. Same battalion. Same regiment. Same division.

Truth, truth, truth. Who decides?

He enlisted in March. Three months later he was in the desert. 130 degrees. Covered with gear. Knocking down doors, firing at insurgents. My son. My beautiful son.

But he didn't last long, did he? Killed in action. A soldier knocked on our door. My wife fell to her knees. He told us the story. How my son's convoy hit a tripwire. How there was an explosion. How his body was burnt beyond recognition. How the only way they knew it was him was because another soldier grabbed one of his tags. And he gave me that tag. Placed it right in my hand. A souvenir of his death.

The stranger stopped speaking and stared at me. The anger in his eyes had been replaced by sadness, by resignation. Finally I spoke because I couldn't take the oppressive silence. I still don't understand. What does all this have to do with me?

His eyes narrowed and his upper lip twitched. He started nodding his head over and over again; I wasn't sure he would ever stop. He said: You showed me a dog tag back at the landfill.

Yeah? So?

Corrosion

What happened to your other tag?

What are you talking about?

Come on, Joseph, or whatever the fuck your name is. You know that every soldier is issued a pair of tags.

I shook my head, said, I lost the other one.

The hell you did!

The stranger grabbed a hold of my hand and shoved something inside of it. I sat there for a long moment, gripping the piece of metal tightly. Then, slowly, I loosened my fingers and stared into the palm of my hand.

A dog tag. Downs. Joseph. My past corroding, my hands trembling, I removed the tag from my neck and compared it to the one in my hand.

They were identical.

There's been a mistake, I said.

He shoved the shotgun in the center of my forehead. No mistake. It took me a while, took some investigating, but now I know what happened. I know —

You don't know shit, I said.

Adrenaline took over. Next thing I knew, I was struggling for the gun and then there was an explosion that deafened my ears. For a moment I thought I was dead. I was wrong. My hands were gripping either end of the shotgun. We fought, and his face was panicked and the veins were popping in his neck. I was younger and stronger than him and eventually I managed to shove the weapon against his throat. He pushed back, but his muscles and will began to weaken. He wasn't able to breathe and his eyes were bulging, his face turning purple. Eventually, his hands loosened from the shotgun. I managed to get some space. I pulled the shotgun back, aimed it at his face and squeezed the trigger. Blood and brain splattered on the windows and on my shirt. The devil was dead, and I was a few steps closer to home.

*   *   *

I sat there for a long time, listening to the blood roaring in my ears. I knew who I was.

There was a shovel in the bed of my truck. I turned my headlights on and stepped outside. The snow was whipping all around me. I walked away from the road and started digging. The ground was cold and hard and the digging was difficult. It must have taken me thirty minutes or more before I'd dug a shallow grave. I was sweating despite the cold. I limped back to the car and pulled open the truck door. Death and destruction. Placing my hands beneath his arms, I managed to pull the stranger out of the pickup. He wasn't heavy, and I dragged him across the snow and toward the grave, rolling him the final few yards into his resting place. Breathing heavily, wiping snow from my brow, I covered him with mud and snow and then got down on my knees and prayed to Jesus Christ with all of my might.

*   *   *

I got into the truck and drove. Tammy Wynette was singing about standing by her man. The wheat fields around me were engulfed in blackness. As the headlights plowed through the darkness, I kept worrying that I might disappear. Off in the distance, the unblinking headlights of a semi appeared, pulling toward me so deliberately that I wondered if I'd ever reach them. Then suddenly they were upon me, and I shielded my eyes with my hand. My Chevy trembled as the big rig rushed past. I watched in my rearview mirror as the red taillights got smaller and smaller, fading into nothingness. Then I was alone again. That ancient coldness rose up inside of me, quickly, unexpectedly. I could barely breathe. I jammed on the brakes, and the car screeched to a halt. I turned off the headlights and the world disappeared. Suddenly, I got the strange sensation that I was staring at the back of my own head.

Panicked, I got out of the pickup, leaving the driver's-side door open and the engine running. I was standing on County Road 13 staring into endless miles of nothingness. I began running down the highway like a fool, just running as hard as I could, not knowing if I could be with myself anymore.

*   *   *

Back in Stratton. All the streets were silent and still, save the dead leaves marching toward their graves. Off to the south the factory smokestacks shot columns of soot into the filthy sky, a human sacrifice to God. I drove down Main Street, stopped at a liquor store. My clothes were covered with blood. I walked inside, zombielike. The windows were barred, and the man behind the register watched me suspiciously as I found the cheapest pint of gin. I paid for the booze, twisting off the top as I staggered outside. Then I sat in my truck and drank. I drank a lot. My head was bobbing around, my tongue lolling outside of my mouth. The devil's shotgun rested on my lap. I weaved through town. I knew where I was going, but I didn't know what I was going to do. My name was Joseph Downs and I came from a small town in Ohio. I was wounded in Mosul when our Humvee exploded. I knew who I was.

* * *

I parked at the edge of her property and turned off the engine. My truck was hidden in the shadow of an old juniper tree. The windows of the little ranch house were glowing orange, the curtains pulled closed. Every so often I could see the silhouette of a woman, then the silhouette of a man, walking through the empty hallway.

I turned on the radio and listened to a Southern preacher, and he got me good and scared. The moon was an evil grin in a basalt sky.

Nobody left the house that night. I watched as the lights began shutting off. First the kitchen. Then the living room. Finally, the bedroom. The whole house was dark. I choked down one last drink, squeezed my eyes shut, and went to sleep.

* * *

Early the next morning I saw him. Tall, thick, ruggedly handsome. The *vaquero* from the bar. He was wearing blue jeans tucked into roper boots, along with a brown Carhartt jacket. He stood outside a while, just gazing across the desolation toward a lonely windmill, the metal blades and tail vane shining all purple and pink and orange in the hazy winter sun. He started walking slowly toward his car, whistling a tune I'd never heard. Then he got inside and hit the engine. I could hear the muffled sounds of Los Ponchos playing from his radio. He put the car into gear and drove, passing right in front of me, kicking up dirt and dust.

Some time passed. I stepped outside of the truck, the snow crunching beneath my bloodstained boots. A bedroom light flashed on, and I saw Lilith in the window. She was wearing a long white gown and her face was otherworldly. I stood in front of my hearse, the shotgun dangling from my hand, a steel appendage. Somewhere in the distance a lonesome train whistle blew. I pulled back my hair with my hand and started walking slowly toward her door. And now I knew what I was going to do, what I had to do. Choices aren't made. There is no free will.

PART TWO:
BENTON FAULK (2003)

"There was something terrible in me sometimes
at night I could see it grinning at me I could see it
through them grinning at me through their faces it's
gone now and I'm sick…"
— William Faulkner, *The Sound and the Fury*

CHAPTER 14

The old man kept the rats in the cellar, hundreds of them in metal cages on cinder block shelves. It was some sight to see, boy, all those rabid rats watching you from beneath those beady black eyes, longing to stick their disease-infested teeth into your flesh. And in the middle of the cellar, a large rectangular table with beakers and Bunsen burners and medicine droppers and notebooks filled with equations and whatnot and all the mountain folk talked and said what's he up to down there, he can't be up to no good, but it didn't bother me even a single bit because Dad knew some things and I trusted him more than all the doctors with their sighs and shaking heads.

And now, as Mother lay in bed in her moth-bitten white nightgown, muscles withering, voice shrieking, Father showed me the Christ Rat, in a cage by itself, body calm, eyes alert, and said, three days, my boy, and no symptoms. Just a little mixture of Tetra-benazine and Peroxetine. An antidote from God himself! Don't know why I didn't think of it sooner! And then I realized how much Father's eyes resembled those of the rats, but still I didn't want to believe all the things the men at the store were saying, didn't want to believe that the Castle was waiting for him. And me upstairs, pacing like one of those caged rats, feeling more than a little melancholy, hoping nobody would come check up on me because the living area was a mess with clothes and blankets and pillows and cans and plates, and they might say enough of this, time to call social services on you! They might say time to put you in a foster family or worse! I walked across the living room, floorboards creaking beneath my graveyard boots, and pulled open the curtains, stared outside. The snow was all over the mountain and it made me realize how cold the house was, colder than a penguin's left nut as they say, so I began gathering wood from the corner of the room and placing it in the fireplace, and by the time the flames were dancing I felt tired and I rested on the couch and snorted some snuff and then fell asleep. Then I was awake again and my head was aching and I could hear my father singing mournful songs and sobbing and I knew he'd sneaked some of that homemade bourbon again, that will be the death of you, I told him once and he just smiled and said better to die from a bad liver than a broken heart and I laughed and said so true, Dad, so true.

Feeling restless and maybe a little anxious, I went to the closet and grabbed my flannel jacket, thinking maybe I'll just get outside, maybe I'll go explore in the mountains and the caves, but I'd just gotten my right arm in the sleeve when I heard my mother's voice, weakened but still shrill, calling out my name, Benton...Benton...Benton. For a moment I thought about ignoring her, but then the guilt stifled me, and I walked slowly toward the bedroom, where the stink of disease seeped from beneath the wooden door.

I stood outside the bedroom for a while hoping she'd stop calling for me, but she was tenacious, so I pushed open the door and stood there, hands useless at my side, eyes aimed downward. I could hear her breathing noisily and I felt sick to my stomach and feared that I'd vomit.

I'm not well, she said, though I'd heard it a million times before, for years and years. I don't have long to live, Benton. Soon I'll be gone and nobody will care. They'll put me in a cheap casket and bury me beneath the dirt, and those worms will have quite a feast, don't you think? And what about you? When I'm dead and buried, will you care?

And when I said that I would, that I loved her because she was my mother and spent sixteen hours giving birth to me, she just laughed and laughed and called me a liar and said she didn't really blame me, that she'd been a terrible mother, unfaithful to me and my father, and once she was dead I should just forget about her, shouldn't bother wasting love on her because there's only so much love in the world, and it's much better to spend it on somebody who can be redeemed.

Then she asked me to sit with her and those were always the words I dreaded to hear, not because I didn't love her, but because I didn't like being near disease, was afraid it might seep under my own skin.

She sat up, her head propped with pillows. Her face was gray, ashen, waxy, her eyes sunken. Her mouth was contorted into a forever scowl, and it was only her hair, long and flowing and black, that looked like my real mother's. Her bare arms rested above the quilt, but they were covered with strange-looking scars.

I didn't want to look at her so I stared at the steel cross hanging from the wall. The doctors are stumped, she said. I don't blame them. The devil gave me this ailment. There are parasites crawling beneath my skin!

I told her that she'd be okay, that Dad would figure something out, that Dad's medicinal punch was working just fine on the Christ Rat, and it would work just fine on her too.

She only grunted and then asked me how school was. I didn't tell her that I hadn't been going because I knew that would break her heart. Instead I told her that I was getting straight A's, that I was on the debate team, that I was on the football team. I told her that scholarships looked likely—oh, you should see me dodge those would-be tacklers!—and I told her that I was dating a pretty young girl who loved Jesus and horses and we were going to get married. Well, Mother was thrilled about that! She started crying, and they were tears of joy, and she said, I always knew you were special, from the very first moment I laid eyes on you!

I sat with her for a while, and she held my hand, and I wished she would fall asleep so I could leave. But she didn't fall asleep and so after a while I said that I had to go, that I had to study, and Mom said she was so proud of me and she hoped I would come visit her again soon, before it was too late, before she'd withered into nothing.

Then I left the house and the snow was falling and I was shivering. I was sixteen but I didn't have a car so I had to walk everywhere, and in the summer it wasn't so bad, but the winter was cold and miserable. I walked down a dirt path and I could see smoke billowing from all the chimneys and just then Old Man Skinner appeared from behind a rusted Ford pickup carrying a load of wood in each arm, and I waved my hand and said how do you do sir, but he just growled and kept right on walking. I was used to that, neighbors judging me on factors beyond my control, that's the way it had always been, but there's no use complaining about that.

By the time I made it to Gold Street, my feet were blocks of ice, my skull crushed and aching. Gold Street wasn't much of a street, more like a dirt road really, but there was a school and a church and a general store and a café, and it was called the Miner's Café and that's where I liked to go from time to time because Constance Durban was a waitress there and sometimes she would wink at me. I blew on my hands and pushed open the door, and nobody was inside except for Eli Wyatt behind the counter, his long white hair combed back into a ponytail, his ruddy face concealed by a decade-old beard, and I wondered when Constance would be there, or if today was her day off, but I didn't say anything because I didn't want to draw suspicion from Eli, didn't want him saying: what are you interested in someone like her for, why she's old enough to be your mother! So instead I looked at the pastries and sandwiches beneath the glass and tried to look as natural as I could. Eli said how ya' doing, Benton Faulk, while wiping the countertop with a rag. Ain't you supposed to be in school?

I told him no, told him all about how my mama was sick and that my father needed me to stay home and help, but I didn't mention the Christ Rat, and Wyatt just nodded his head in sympathy and said it sure is a shame that Catherine is sick. I said indeed it is, then asked for a root beer, not the one from the fountain but the one in the bottle with the old-time writing on it, and he nodded his head slowly, wiped his hands on his apron, and pulled out a bottle from the cooler. He opened it for me and poured it into a frosted mug, then asked if I wanted a slice of cherry pie, that it would be on the house, and I said, I sure do appreciate it, that pie looks awfully good. And it did look good—you could see the cherries bursting out of the crust, and I could just tell they'd be juicy and sweet.

So I sat all alone at the end of a long metal picnic table and sipped the root beer and ate the cherry pie and watched the snow fall. Then, a few minutes past five, the door to the café opened and Constance Durban entered and she already looked tired and haggard even though her shift hadn't started, but I thought she was the most beautiful woman in the world. She was tall, maybe a little on the heavy side, and had bright red hair. When she saw me, she gave me that secret wink, and I'm here to tell you, my heart jumped like a jackrabbit with a firecracker up its ass, as they say.

I watched her as she tied her apron, watched her as she wiped a wisp of hair from her face, watched her as she joked with Eli Wyatt, watched her as she walked toward her customers, smacking on gum, flipping through her notepad.

And for the next hour or more I drank root beer after root beer until my stomach ached and every once in a while she'd glance my way and for a moment things weren't so rotten and I didn't think about Mom's disease and Dad's rats and my life.

CHAPTER 15

During those days, I spent a lot of time reading, only it wasn't any school books, it was a comic book called *Fight to the Finish,* and it featured the Soldier, a kick-ass motherfucker who wouldn't hesitate to blow up every last Arab if it meant making America a safer place to live. He didn't play by the rules and when the other soldiers were hiding in their barracks, the Soldier would gladly walk into a mosque filled with jihadists and give each one of them sons-of-bitches a bullet to the brain, and there wouldn't be 72 virgins waiting for them, I can tell you that much. But he wasn't just a destroyer, he had a heart of gold too, like when he saved that little Iraqi boy from the crumbling building, now how many soldiers would do that, not too many if you ask me!

I figured I'd enlist in the army just as soon as I turned eighteen, figured I'd get the hell out of Silverville and go off and fight all those terrorists in the desert and I'd be sure to write home to Constance: Dear Constance, I hope things are good with you, Iraq is hard to describe, there's a lot of carnage. Just the other day we drove down the highway and I saw a dead Iraqi woman in a car, eyes wide open, mouth frozen in a silent scream. Seems like all I do is wait and worry about getting killed, but I hope you're happy in Silverville and I hope little Timmy is doing well. Tell him I'll be home soon, God willing, I love the both of you more than life itself!

Meanwhile, the old man remained hard at work in the basement, poking the rats with needles, mumbling results into his tape recorder: Morphological and electrophysiological alterations in striatum and cortex. Reduced membrane capacitance and increased input resistance in neurons from symptomatic mice. Decreases in somatic size, dendritic field, and cortical pyramidal neurons. And the Christ Rat, in a cage by itself, symptom free for nearly a week.

As for Mother, she was now just a series of tics, the beginning stages of chorea. Her jaw was clenched, her speech was slurred, and swallowing was difficult. When she spoke, it was confusing and I couldn't always follow. When she cried, it was the sobbing of a little girl, and I cried too while the blackened lodgepoles swayed menacingly out the window.

Dr. Tanner came to examine my mother. He wore an oversized gray suit and had an oversized gray beard. He carried an oak-tanned leather Upjohn medicine bag but I doubted anything was inside. He entered my mother's room jovially, joking with my father, laughing Ed McMahon-style. My father, hunched over like Quasimodo, mumbled on and on about Tetrabenazine and Peroxetine, but the doctor paid him no mind.

They were in that room for a long time. I could hear my mother screaming and I sat in a rocking chair and thought about cherry pie and root beer and Constance Durban. And then the doctor and my father came out and the doctor wasn't laughing anymore. He spoke to my father in hushed tones, and he squeezed my shoulder and told me to take good care of myself, and I remembered when Mother was healthy and the world was less sad.

An hour later, I was inside Lucky's Liquors chatting up old Henderson, the fellow with the golf ball goiter. I told him that I needed to get a bottle of whiskey for the old man, but he wasn't buying it. He said: I'm not going to risk losing my liquor license for a little punk like you and he laughed like he was just joking, but I knew that he wasn't. I told him no hard feelings, that I'd just tell Dad to come down to the liquor store and get the bottle his own lazy self, and the Goiter seemed satisfied, and I waited until he turned his head and then I grabbed a bottle of something and stuck it under my shirt and said, well, I'll be seeing you around, Mr. Henderson, hope it doesn't snow too hard tonight.

When I got outside, I looked at the label on the bottle: Jelínek's plum brandy. I unscrewed the top and took a long swig. It tasted terrible, but after a few more drinks I started to get used to it and then I started to feel better and the frigid air started to feel warmer.

Well, I got a little drunk and I wandered through

Silverville, by all the cabins and shacks, and I was singing Christmas songs and stumbling over fallen branches and laughing at some secrets.

And I must have been distracted because soon I was deep in the mountains and maybe a little bit lost and the rain was falling and the wind was blowing. I didn't panic because I knew that the worst thing that could happen was that I'd die and that wasn't much worse than my present state of being, so I kept walking and kept singing, but now my singing was slower and softer.

And then an amazing thing happened. In the middle of nowhere, I came across an old collapsed mine and then just a little farther I saw a little mining cabin and I had the very strange sensation that I'd been there before, that I'd lived there before, maybe in another life, in another century, and the things that I'd done there were terrible. Slowly I walked to the cabin and I felt scared but then I thought about the Soldier and I grabbed a walking stick and pretended it was a rifle and shouted out: All right, you piece of shit towel heads, come on out with your hands held high or I swear by the real God that I'll blow you straight to Kingdom Come! But there was no answer except the wind and the rain, so I stepped inside the shack and there was dust everywhere and there was a wood-burning stove and a gas lantern and a busted chair and a small cot. Next to the fireplace was a brush and a shovel and a poker, all a hundred years old at least. I walked back and forth across the shack, the floor sounding like dead leaves beneath my feet, and then terrible images started bouncing around my skull at breakneck speed and I felt scared again and this time the Soldier couldn't do a damn thing to make me feel better. So I left that shack but I knew for certain that I'd be back. It was my new hideaway and nobody would know about it, not ever, except maybe for Constance, I'd tell her anything.

Well, it took me a good long while, but eventually I did manage to find my way back home but I wished I hadn't because when I got inside, my father was sitting in the kitchen all by himself, drinking bourbon, his head in his hands, a man defeated. I stood in the doorway and said is everything okay, Dad, you're looking a little green. He looked up and shook his head and pulled his right hand from his lap and that's when I knew that hope was dwindling fast because he was gripping a rat and it was dead and it was the Christ Rat.

CHAPTER 16

Dad wouldn't dispose of the Christ Rat because he was waiting for its resurrection. Meanwhile, the bedroom door stayed locked and there was no way of getting in and don't think I didn't try! Oftentimes I could hear the old man behind the door sobbing and praying and I knew it was pretty bad because Dad never prayed, at least not that I knew of, and he wouldn't let me see her, wouldn't let me see my own mother. If you ask me to tell you the God's honest truth, I think he'd given up on finding a cure, because his basement laboratory stayed untouched and those rats were left to fend for themselves. Rats can only survive for so long without food before they resort to cannibalism, but that's no different from you and me if we're really honest with ourselves.

And each time he came out of the room I pleaded with him to let me see Mother, that it had been weeks since I'd been in her room, but the old man wasn't having any of it. She's sick, can't you see? The more you bother her, the sicker she's going to get! You just mind your own business, you hear?

And meanwhile, a woman whose name I didn't recognize kept calling and telling me that I sure better start attending school or else social services would come and that would be the end of me, so I made up my mind to give it a chance, not forever, but just for long enough to get this awful woman off my back. Of course, I hadn't been to school in some time, and I worried that my teachers wouldn't even know who I was, but I shouldn't have worried about that, no sir! They all knew my name, they all knew my story, and they all seemed put out that I was back, like I was making their lives extra difficult. Well, it's been a long time, Benton Faulk, said the teacher with the bird nose and dandruff-covered sports jacket, and I agreed it had been a long time. I've been caring for my ill mother, I said. I'm so sorry to hear that and blather, blather, blather.

So I sat in the back of each of my classes and it was a terrible experience, I tell you, because I have no interest in sine and cosine, or subjects and pronouns, or World War I and World War II. And at lunch I had nobody to sit next to and then I saw a few kids that I knew from way back when: Edward Kelly with his Polo shirt and arrogant grin; Tanner Fitzgerald with his military buzz and faggot lisp; Billy Gallegos with his acned face and dull-eyed stare. Do you mind if I sit here, I said holding a tray of meat loaf and apple sauce and chocolate milk, and they all looked at each other and laughed nervously, and then I started laughing too, and it was like we were sharing a great big fat joke, the four of us buddies from way back when. And that gave me an idea. I started telling them the jokes that I knew, just to see if I could keep the moment going. Said I: Did you know that the average tit weighs a pound and a half? Well, it's true! And do you know how much a pussy weighs? They were stumped, absolutely stumped. Well, Billy, I said, why don't you go step on a scale, and we'll find out!

Yeah, that was a funny one, but none of them thought so, and after a short while they left the table, so it was just me sitting by myself and soon I decided that I wasn't feeling hungry anymore so I dumped my tray and left the cafeteria and sneaked out of the building and didn't come back the next day or the day after that.

*   *   *

But I spent a lot of time at the Miner's Café, and Constance was more than a little bit nice to me. She had heard about my mother—news travels quickly in small towns—and she told me that she was so sorry, told me that she knew what I was going through, that she had lost someone not so long ago, and that her heart hurt every second of every day. And she had a locket around her neck that she squeezed and I wondered what picture was inside and then her eyes turned moist and red because she was sad thinking about loss and whatnot and I got my courage up and asked her if she wanted to go out and get a drink sometime, that she was the prettiest and kindest woman in all of Silverville, but she thought that Little Benton was just joking and she wiped away the tears and smiled a little and then walked away, her body swaying slowly.

And the minutes seemed like hours and the hours like days, and at some point it dawned on me that it would be a good idea to find out where Constance lived, so one day I waited until she finished work and cashed out her tips and then I followed her, staying a ways back, ducking behind trees now and then, and it turned out she lived nearby because she didn't even have to drive, and if she had seen me, I would have said, Oh, hi, Ms. Durban, I was just on my way home, wasn't following you, wasn't following you at all!

She lived in a little log cabin buried in the woods. I watched as she reached beneath a mat and pulled out a key and unlocked the door, and then I crouched behind a pine tree all covered with powdered sugar and waited and watched and waited some more. I thought about my mother and the Soldier and the Christ Rat and that got me good and emotional and I started crying just like a goddamn little girl, and I couldn't stop, and then I looked up and saw an orange glow from behind the curtain, and I stopped crying, and then I heard the sound of a piano, soft and lovely, and I imagined her sitting on the couch listening to the music, thinking of love, thinking of me. I watched the cabin for a long time, hoping against hope that she'd pull back that curtain, and Jesus must have been looking out for me, because eventually she did open the curtain and I could see her standing there, gazing into the darkness and cold, the same piano piece playing for the third time at least. She wore a yellow nightgown and her red hair was long and straight and beautiful. I pulled her close, wiped a tear from her eye, and said, nobody's going to hurt you anymore, Constance, I promise you that much. Oh, Benton, she said. I just can't stand it anymore. This world is such a terrible place! I kissed her lips, soft and sweet. We'll leave it behind, I said. Every last drop of sadness and meanness. We'll leave it behind. Then the curtains closed and the music stopped and she was gone and I started crying again, goddamn it all to hell.

*   *   *

And now I should tell you about Horace Faulk because he plays a major role in this story, and not in a good way as you might have guessed. He was my dad's brother, which made him my uncle. He was tall and serious and religious and had a mustache. My father didn't much like him and he didn't much like my father. I didn't know him well enough to have an opinion, but typically I don't have a problem with people unless they're scheming to get me or my dad.

Well, this one morning he stood on the front porch, pounding on the door, calling out my dad's name, peeping in the window like a goddamn Tom. My father was off somewhere and my mother was locked in her room, so it was just me and my bad thoughts, as they say. The old man would later tell me on numerous occasions to not let that self-righteous bastard inside, but at this point I hadn't heard his warnings and so I opened the door, figuring family, family.

He wore a suit and a tie even though he didn't have a dollar and a job, and he said, Hi there, Benton, buddy, how are things?

Well, I wasn't sure if he was trying to trick me by acting all kind and polite, trying to get some top secret information out of me, so I didn't answer, didn't say anything at all.

Where's your dad? he said, and it was more of an accusation than a question.

Stiffly: Well, I can't say that I know.

What about your mom?

Resting.

I could tell that Uncle Horace wasn't satisfied, wasn't satisfied at all. He adjusted his tie and smoothed out his mustache and said: I haven't seen her in some time, and frankly I'm a little bit concerned. I've heard some things. Some rumors. Figured I'd check things out.

Like I said, she's resting. She's not well.

But Uncle Horace just stood there studying me with those rat eyes, the same rat eyes as Dad's, and I suddenly had a terrible feeling that he was something terrible and would do something terrible to all of us.

Do you want me to tell her something? I said.

I'd like to tell her myself.

Well, I said, I guess that's not possible. I guess you should be going.

But he didn't go, not for some time, just stood there asking questions, difficult questions, saying that something was not right, saying that the mountain folk were sure starting to talk, saying that my father was sure acting suspicious, and I tuned out what he was saying and imagined that I was the Soldier and I was battle ready, firing my AK-57 with one hand, dragging out the wounded with the other. Shirt torn and bloody, bullet lodged in my shoulder. These are my boys! I'm shouting. They've got homes, families! They ain't dying under my watch!

Want me to tell you what they're saying? Uncle Horace asked.

Not interested, I said. Don't care. They don't know us. They don't know who we really are.

You're wrong, boy. *You* don't know who you really are.

And that got me thinking, because it was a philosophical statement for sure, how we don't ever really know who we are, how we let ourselves be defined by our enemies, and eventually Uncle Horace left but not before he scolded me some more and told me we'd better clean up our house, because it was sure a disgrace. But I didn't tell him a thing about the the Christ Rat and his coming resurrection, because he would have used that against my father and they would have dragged him to the Castle with all the screaming and wailing and moaning and screaming…

CHAPTER 17

And then there was the smell. I didn't notice it right away but that was probably because it happened gradually like when fruit sits in a hot kitchen for too long, not all of a sudden like when somebody takes a crap in your living room. And by the time I did notice the smell, I guess you could say it was too late because Dad was too far gone to do anything about it, and Mother was not well, what with the way the disease had ravaged her body, and the last thing that I wanted to do was go to the basement and deal with the dead Christ Rat and all his prophets because I hated rats—did you know they can go for twenty days without sleeping and their teeth never stop growing and some rats grow to eight pounds, did you know that?

So I spent most of my time outside of the house and I went to school sometimes, and I watched Constance when I could. Nobody understood what I felt for her, not even Constance herself. I knew that I would never let her go and if anybody gave me a hard time, I would show them a thing or two because now I was carrying a knife in my jacket pocket—an old Browning hunter with a gut hook.

And when I was feeling at my lowest, when I felt like I was ready to explode, I would hike out in the mountains and get away to my new sanctuary, the old mining cabin. I called it the Skull Shack—death to anybody who entered and that kind of stuff. I was loading the place up with canned food and blankets and knives and pillows and back issues of *Fight to the Finish*, just in case I needed to go into hiding from all the infidels skulking through Silverville.

There was this one night when the old man stood behind me and I could tell he'd been drinking what with the way he stank of cheap bourbon and cheaper stogies. When I turned around, I saw that his face was all pale and waxy and his mouth was fixed into a terrible grin. He was just a hunchback skeleton, his skull balanced on a wobbly cervical vertebrae. You been sneaking around? he said, his voice quiet and lilting, offering a false sense of comfort. I just shook my head and said, no sir. He placed his bony hand on my shoulder and said, your mother has gotten even sicker. You might not be able to see her for some time still.

Then I was mad and I asked him about the rats and his experiments and had he given up on finding a cure? Was he just going to let her die without a fight? But Dad avoided my question and instead he talked about religion and God. He said: I used to not

believe in him, just thought it was a bunch of super-
stition, that there wasn't an ounce of scientific proof
that I could rely on. But now I'm a changed man.
Now I'm a true believer!

What happened? I asked. What type of revelation
did you have?

Yes, revelation. That's a good word for it, Benton.
The revelation came from seeing what's happened
to your mom, from seeing what's happened to this
world. Now I'm certain that there is a Supreme Being; it's the only explanation. Only he isn't kind and
benevolent, our Lord, he is hateful and malicious,
nothing but an ornery child stomping on an anthill!

And then, without saying another word, he
reached into his shirt pocket and pulled out a bronze
skeleton key and proceeded to unlock and push open
the bedroom door. Sensing an opportunity, I tried entering, tried pushing past him, but he was prepared
for that, and he shoved me backward and slammed
shut the door. And despite my pounding and pleading and sobbing, the door remained locked, and
I didn't see my father for another three days and I
didn't see my mother for another four weeks.

* * *

Well, I'll tell you this: that dead Christ Rat stank.
Yes, he stank so bad, I could hardly see straight, and
every time I'd step into the house, the bile would coat
my throat. You wouldn't have thought an animal that
small could give off such a stench, but I am living
witness that it could, and the proof came when I was
pulled out of class by the school counselor, and she

sat me in her office and said this is a very difficult subject to broach but there have been several complaints made by other students about your personal hygiene and, in particular, about your odor, and I have to agree with them, you certainly do smell, Benton, you smell something awful. And they dragged me out of school kicking and screaming, and said don't you dare come back until you've sterilized yourself in some boiling water! And if that episode wasn't proof enough, what about when the little man and his little wife from down the road showed up at our house with their bottles of Lysol, thinking we couldn't see them, spraying like lunatics at the base of the house while my old man stood at the window, pulling the curtains back so he could watch them, mumbling beneath his whiskey breath: They'll get what's coming to 'em, that they will.

And then the stench faded, but I guess the suspicions did not, because one snowy morning, a few weeks later, Uncle Horace came knocking at our door, and I'm here to tell you that they were the loneliest three knocks you ever did hear. The old man was sitting on the couch, sipping on bourbon, reading a dog-eared copy of the *American Journal of Medicine*, while I was illustrating my own version of *Fight to the Finish*, involving Constance Durban as a hostage forced to do terrible things by the Arabs before the Soldier cuts all their throats and rescues her. When he heard the knocking, my dad looked up slowly and stared at that door for a long time. Then he nodded at me, said, open the door, young man. It's about time we had a visitor.

I was feeling uneasy, but what else could I do but

follow the old man's orders? Horace Faulk stood on the porch wearing that same tattered suit as before. His mustache was thicker and bushier than last time, and the rest of his face was in need of a shave. He was wearing gold-rimmed spectacles that rested on the tip of his narrow nose. His graying hair was wild and unruly. In his bony hands he held a leather-bound book, which I do believe was a King James Bible. I didn't say a thing, just stood there, blocking Uncle Horace from entering. Hello, again, Benton. I'd like to speak with your father.

I told him no because my father had warned me about letting the self-righteous bastard inside, but he was dogged and refused to move from the porch. That's when the old man rose to his feet, his face half-hidden by shadows. He took a couple of steps forward, shielding his eyes from the daylight. His upper lip rose into a snarl of hatred. What do you want, Horace? I don't believe that you're all that welcome in my house.

Where is she, Flan?

Where is who?

Catherine.

She's sick.

How sick?

Sick.

Then Father grinned and it was an awful grin, and he said, she's so sick that you might not ever get to place your filthy fingers inside of her again.

Uncle Horace shook his head. I never touched your wife.

That's not what I heard.

You're crazy, Flan. You need help.

I think it'd be best if you left now, Dad said. But Uncle Horace took a step forward and tried peering into the living room. Dad sensed his aim and hobbled over to block him. Get the hell away from my property or I'll call the sheriff. And Uncle Horace might have listened to his warning, might have turned around and walked away, but then his eyes came to rest on the wooden mantel where the sun reflected off Mom's diamond engagement ring.

Now I guess the sight of the ring must have stirred some new suspicions inside of Uncle Horace, because despite the old man's warnings, he took another step forward and then another. Dad suddenly seemed weak and old, and he said, just leave me be, please just leave me be. But Horace looked up at him with hatred in his eyes and then reached back with his arm and lunged forward, his open palm connecting with Dad's face. It wasn't much of a blow, but Dad wasn't expecting it, I can tell you that much, because he tripped over his own feet and went tumbling onto the hardwood floor, jaw bouncing. Without waiting another moment, Horace staggered into the house toward the bedroom, and he'd almost reached it when the old man recovered, got to his knees, grabbed him by the ankle and pulled him down. Then he placed his bony red hands around his throat and started squeezing harder and harder, trying, I do believe, to kill his own brother.

While my father was struggling with Horace, I noticed that the room key had fallen out of the old man's trouser pocket and I was overcome by morbid curiosity. I snatched the key off the floor and walked slowly to the bedroom, which you can hardly blame

Corrosion

me for doing because I hadn't seen my mother in such a long time.

I unlocked the door and pushed it open and then I wished I hadn't because she was lying on the canopy bed, naked, her hands held stiffly at her side, her once beautiful black hair fallen in clumps on the pillow. Flies and maggots were crawling on her darkened body, her eyes were just empty sockets, and I was laughing and screaming and praying all at once.

Corrosion

me for doing because I hadn't seen my mother in such a long time.

I unlocked the door and pushed it open and then I wished I hadn't because she was lying on the canopy bed, naked, her hands held stiffly at her side, her once beautiful black hair fallen in clumps on the pillow. Flies and maggots were crawling on her darkened body, her eyes were just empty sockets, and I was laughing and screaming and praying all at once.

128

CHAPTER 18

The moon shattered into a million pieces and Father plotted his move, saying, if they think they can prevent a man from going to his own wife's funeral, if they think they can prevent a man from mourning in the proper way, they've got another thing coming! I'll be damned if I allow them to turn me into some sort of pariah when all I did, all I ever did, was love and honor. It was my life's work finding a cure for that woman, my life's work! And that after she had fornicated with my brother and all the rest of them. Still, I loved and honored. And what did all the rest of them do for her, tell me that? Well, I'll tell you. I'll tell you exactly what they did for her: not a goddamn thing! And now they're going to try and punish me? And now they're going to say, well Flan Faulk, it's time you stay home, it's time you stay away, we'll take care of the burial, yes we will? Well, I'll tell you something, Benny Boy, we're not going to go quietly! We're not going to go peacefully!

And I knew better to argue with the old man because when he got his mind made up, he was awful stubborn, so he made his plans and I went right along with them even though I knew it was a mistake, even though I knew it would lead to him being dragged away to the Castle...

* * *

So here's how things looked on this particular December morning: Outside the snow was falling and the mountain was as quiet as a Mormon whorehouse, as they say. I got dressed in my bedroom and then took a look in the mirror at the gangly boy with shoulder-length hair, pale skin, and a hobo suit, and I wanted to laugh, I wanted to break down and laugh, but I knew my father might hear me and take the belt out maybe. Before leaving, I snorted some snuff and drank a healthy portion of newly stolen Jelínek's plum brandy, so I felt stuffed full of fairies and harps and Christmas cheers. I shouted out a good-bye but my father didn't answer; he was in the basement, planning, plotting, plotting.

The church wasn't too far of a walk and I didn't go there much and it was a little brown church in the vale and there were crows roosting on the steeple. Pastor Rucker greeted me at the door of the church and tried embracing me, but I ducked out of the way, and then an old woman tried hugging me too, but I wouldn't let her either saying you think you can turn my father into a pariah and she wore an ankle-length black dress and Benjamin Franklin spectacles and her silver hair was strangled in a bun.

There weren't hardly any people there at all but the ones who were there were staring at me and whispering from behind their hands, and little Peggy Weiss with the Shirley Temple curls tugged at my sleeve and said, gee Benton I sure am sorry about your mother, and I patted her head and said don't worry about me but then when nobody was looking, I leaned down and whispered in her ear: I'm afraid the poor lady had no use for Jesus our savior so now she's burning in the fiery furnaces of hell, and that got little Peggy good and nervous and she drifted back to her seat and I was all alone.

Well, I wasn't sure where to sit so I sat in the back row. An old gentleman wearing suspenders and a bolo tie and an eye patch said boy ya ought to show your respect and sit by the coffin but I figured corpses have no use for manners so I stayed right where I was and outside the lightning was flashing and the thunder was rolling and if you were a true believer, you might have thought God was thumping his chest a bit.

Pastor Rucker waited for a while, hoping more would show up, but they never did, so he stood at the lectern and raised his hands to the heavens and said in a booming voice: We are here to honor the life of Catherine Faulk and give thanks to the eternal life that awaits her. Yes, it is true. Catherine has returned home. Yes, it is true. By dying, Christ vanquished death. By rising, Christ restored our life. Please understand: the death of a Christian should not be a time for mourning. You see, the death of a Christian is a wonderful thing. Why then do we cry? Why then do we gnash our teeth? Why then do we think of death as an enemy? Suppose you were a prisoner of war and you were tortured every day, you were whipped with strips cut from rubber tires until the skin on your back hung in shreds. Then suppose a soldier busted down that door and vanquished the persecutors and rescued you from that agony and took you to a place of slumber and fine food and joy. Wouldn't you consider this rescuer as a good friend? Then why not death? Why not Christ?

And the ladies who were there pulled out their handkerchiefs and dabbed their eyes and said: Amen! Yes, death is a good friend! Yes, Jesus is a good friend! He cares for us, yes he does!

And the pastor kept right on talking, face beet-red, fists pounding on the lectern. Yes, my brethren, in life we only have an incomplete enjoyment of God, in death we have a perfect enjoyment of him! The glorious things of heaven are so many that they exceed estimation, so great that they exceed measure! Here in this present world, we receive grace, but in heaven we receive glory. He who tries to see God here on earth sees only a silhouette, but through death we see his face, a jewel of splendor! Death is another Moses, delivering us out of bondage and persecution. Death is the Christian's wedding day, a rest from sin, from sadness, from temptations, from illness! A Christian's last day is, my friends, her best day, a day of triumph and exaltation, a day of freedom and consolation, a day of rest and satisfaction! And bowing his head, softening his voice, the Pastor said: And now let us pray.

And I bowed my head, just like everybody else, but I didn't pray for even a second. Instead I thought about what a load of crap it all was, every last word of it, and I wished they could just face the facts, I wished they could just face the reality. And that was this: Death was no friend of Dad's. Death was no friend of mine. And Death was no friend of Mother's.

So the church was quiet and Mother's casket was at the front and I wondered what her body looked like now. Had they preserved her, sutured her face together, filled her eye sockets with cotton balls, pumped embalming fluid in her arteries? Or had they let her decay naturally, a mountain of putrefaction?

Yes, the church was quiet. But then the wooden door swung open and everybody looked up, whiskey drinkers in a B-Western saloon. My father stood in the doorway, wearing his lab coat and pajama bottoms, holding an oversized cage in each hand. And stuffed inside those cages, with hardly room to move, gnawing at each other's limbs, screeching and hollering, ready to attack, were a million and one disease-infested rats.

CHAPTER 19

The old man kneeled down and he had a big sideways grin on his face, and he opened the cages, and for a few moments nothing happened—the rats must have been suspicious of being granted freedom, thought it was too good to be true—but Dad nudged a couple of them, and pretty soon they started marching in unison, the Rats Liberation Army, and their noses were twitching, and then they left their posts and began scurrying up toward the altar, attracted maybe to the familiar odor of Mother's rotted flesh. For a long while there was no reaction from the congregation—it must have taken a few moments for all the synapses to connect, for people to make sense of what was happening—then there were a few gasps and a few murmurs and finally a blood-curdling scream from Donna Gallegos, that ugly hag with the wart-infested cheek, and that was the start of holy pandemonium, the likes of which I had not seen for some time.

Rats! Rats! they all screamed and pretty soon everybody was out of their seats tap-dancing and hollering, acting like this was Eleventh Plague of Egypt, and the pastor kept right on preaching, saying what a friend we have in Jesus, all our sins and griefs to bear, what a privilege to carry everything to God in prayer, but nobody was listening, they were pushing and shoving, trying to escape the century-old church, and pretty soon there were people on the ground, children, the elderly, and they were being trampled over, and my old man was laughing and slapping his thigh in delight, and then he motioned to me and said: March onward, Christian soldier! but my ligaments and tendons were all ruptured so I couldn't move even an inch. In frustration, he moved next to me, grabbed my arm, squeezing tight, and started pulling. C'mon, boy, he said, it's time for phase two!

And everybody was going one way and we were going the other way and only Pastor Rucker and a few other stalwarts remained to protect the corpse and possibly the bodily resurrection of my mother, a woman who never prayed, a woman who enjoyed sin as much as grace, and my father said, okay boy you take one end and I'll take the other, and everything was a blur, but soon we were carrying the coffin, thieves in the House of the Lord, and it was heavier than you might think, and then a couple of men were grabbing at Dad, and a couple more were grabbing at me, and the coffin fell to the ground, and it opened, and Mom was still dead, still rotting, still hideous, and they took Dad away, took Dad far away, walking with him slowly down the corridor, arm-in-arm-in-arm, shoving him into a white padded room with only a mattress and a Bible and a flickering fluorescent light and the rats scampered through the pipes, and Dad's eyes were empty, and he rocked back and forth, yanked out clumps of hair, scratched at the floors, bit through his lip, screamed at the top of his lungs, gibberish all, swatted at imaginary flies, laughed the laughter of a lunatic, and he was in the Castle.

*   *   *

I was still a year away from being able to live on my own, so they placed me with Uncle Horace and Aunt Rose and for a long time I wouldn't talk to them, I would just sit in my bedroom and read about the Soldier and bite the skin off my knuckles. Uncle Horace did his best, sitting me down and saying, this is your home now. I know you've been through a lot, but you're safe here with Aunt Rose and me. And after a while I started talking again, but I never talked about Dad or Mom and soon it was like they'd never been here at all.

Things were sure different at my uncle and aunt's house. We said grace before meals and couldn't wear hats inside the house, and they wanted me to pray and accept Jesus into my heart and I told them that I would, I told them that I believed that Jesus was the Savior and that he would save me from my sins and both Uncle Horace and Aunt Rose were so happy, Aunt Rose even cried good long tears, and I was thankful to have a nice house to live in, and there were no rats and no odors.

Due to my aunt's nagging, I went back to school some of the time and throughout all of these ups and downs I didn't hardly think about Constance the Waitress at all, but then I saw her walking out in the mountains by herself, wearing blue jeans and a flannel jacket, her red hair falling to her waist. She was an Angel of Mercy, a Liberator of Souls, a Messiah of the Heart, and I figured that redemption was a possibility.

I didn't want to scare her and I didn't want to hurt her, but I followed her tracks, the snow crunching beneath my feet. She didn't turn back, deep in thought, maybe. She marched up the mountain path, lodgepoles towering, and I stayed back a ways, careful as always. And Constance continued hiking upward, and the air was getting cooler, and there were rows of boulders and log walls, and there were collapsed mines scattered across the floor like pickup sticks, rotted by centuries of storms.

And after another twenty minutes or more, she stopped, stood there for a few moments, then took to resting on a rock. She pulled out a bottle of water and placed it to her lips, and I stood there hidden in the shadows, watching her, and I got to thinking how the mountain was full of death and snow and ghosts and how I sure would like get off the mountain someday, and how maybe Constance would go with me, how we were both as lonely as any of these abandoned mines dotting the mountainside.

And then I was humming "Teddy Bear" by Red Sovine and walking toward where Constance was sitting, and I never meant to frighten her, but I was standing right behind her, and she thought she was alone, and when she looked back, she gasped and rose to her feet. I said, don't worry, it's just me, Benton Faulk from the diner, and she still looked scared and said, what are you doing here?

Just taking a hike, I said, I hike this way sometimes when I want to clear my head. And she just nodded, but her face was pale and her eyes were wild like a wounded mule deer, and I was angry with myself for sneaking up on her like that, especially here high in the mountains where nobody could hear her scream.

I said, did you hear about the latest with my mother, nasty situation, and she nodded and said that yes she'd heard. My father didn't hurt her, I said, he was trying to save her, and he almost succeeded with the Christ Rat, but then the Christ Rat died, and nobody else cared if she lived or died, they all thought that she was mountain trash, but she wasn't, her great-grandfather made a fortune in silver, owned a dozen or more mines. And once Mom and me walked together to the top of Pewter Hill and the night was cold, and the snow was falling, and the world was quiet, and she took hold of my hand and pointed all around us and said, this is heaven, Benton, don't you ever forget it, and we stood there for a long time, me and my mother, just watching and touching and feeling. And those memories are mine…

And then I was out of words and Constance said that she'd better start heading back down the mountain, and I said, wait a minute, do you want me to show you something, an old abandoned mining cabin, I use it as my hideaway, and nobody else knows about it, but I'll show you, and she said no, that she really needed to be making her way back. So I nodded and told her to be alert, that there were mountain lions and collapsed mines out this way and you had to be careful of such things, that life could end at any moment, a bullet to the heart, a knife to the throat, a club to the head.

I stood in the shadows of the swaying trees and watched her walk back down the path, and she was walking much quicker now, and she looked back a few times, and she didn't smile, and her eyes were still scared, and the snow started falling, and I knew my aunt and uncle would be wondering where I was, but I decided to go to the mining cabin and read about the Soldier and think about my plans for the near future.

CHAPTER 20

Sitting at the dinner table, eating elk stew, Aunt Rose eyeing me suspiciously, Uncle Horace slurping loudly. I didn't speak much when I was with them because there was nothing I could possibly say to them and when they asked me questions, I could always nod my head or shake my head or not respond at all. But I could tell that Rose had something on her mind because she hadn't touched her stew and usually she had three or four portions at least, which went a long ways to explaining her chubby cheeks and enormous bottom. Well, it wasn't until I was getting up, ready to bring my dish to the kitchen sink that she said go on and sit down, Benton, and it took me a few moments because I didn't like the tone of her voice, but then I sat down and waited to hear what she had to say.

Her voice was all full of anxiety and disappointment. She told me that a woman had stopped by just this morning asking to see me, and when she'd asked what this was all about, the woman said that I'd been making her feel uncomfortable, what with the way I'd been talking to her and watching her and so forth. Do you know who this Constance Durban is, Aunt Rose asked. No, ma'am, I said and started to get up because I didn't like where this conversation was headed and I just wanted to read the latest edition of *Fight to the Finish* where the Soldier is caught between a rock and a hard place. But Rose wouldn't let me be. This woman, she said, seemed awfully serious. And she's prepared to call the proper authorities if you keep bothering her. You sure you don't know who Constance Durban is?

Well, I didn't answer *that* question because it was manipulative and sadistic. Instead I threw my bowl on the ground and it shattered and you could tell that my aunt and uncle were surprised about that, elk stew and china all over the place, and I went into my room and read for a while and then I drank some brandy and chewed some tobacco, growing vices both.

What's this all about, I asked Constance, and her eyes were bloodshot and her handkerchief was trembling next to her face. Why'd you come to my house saying all of those terrible things? And I was as mad as could be and I could tell that Constance was plenty frightened. It's my ex-husband, she said. He'd been gone for a long time, but now he's returned to the mountain. And he's possessive. He won't let me go. No matter what I say. No matter what I do. He saw the two of us and he got jealous and now he's making threats, saying, you stop foolin' around with that little boy or I'll skin you like a stuck hog! I didn't want to tell your aunt those things, but I was scared. You're the only one I love, Benton! You're the only one I need!

*   *   *

Back in the Skull Shack I read about the Soldier and how he hid in a rabbit hole for four days and four nights while the Taliban searched for him with crocodile sheers and flaying knives and Spanish ticklers, and the sweat poured from his face, but he never panicked, not for a moment, because he had more mental strength than all the towel heads put together. And then I looked around the cabin and realized that I wasn't safe here, that they could find me and torture me, so I decided right then and there that I needed some sort of a hideout within my hideout and I had a pretty good idea how to make one, but I'd need some tools.

Kyle Weaver was crazy and he was blind too, and he worked with an anvil and a forge fire in a little mountain shack overlooking the river. He'd always liked me, I always put a smile on his face, so when I said I needed a sharpened crosscut saw and a mattock and a shovel, he said, well that's no problem at all AND how are you, I heard you've been through a lot. That's the thing about people. They always meddle when they shouldn't, and that was another good reason to make the root cellar, to keep the meddlers away.

Jon Bassoff

And the work wasn't easy, but I sawed for hours at a time, and I sure am worried about Benton, I could hear Aunt Rose saying, he's acting mighty strange, I haven't heard him say a word in days, and Uncle Horace said, for Christ's sake he's lost his mother and father in the most excruciating way possible, give the boy some time, give the boy some space.

And sometimes I'd go to school, just to keep them off my back, and sometimes I'd hide behind Constance's house, waiting for her old man, but he didn't dare show his face, and some of the time I'd work on my project at the shack. The sawing was done, I'd completed a near-perfect square, and now I was using the mattock and the round-point shovel, and my hands were covered with blisters, I didn't use gloves, and I sang until my voice was hoarse:

> *I'm lonesome since I crossed the hill,*
> *And o'er the moorland sedgy*
> *Such heavy thoughts my heart do fill,*
> *Since parting with my Betsey*
> *I seek for one as fair and gay,*
> *But find none to remind me*
> *How sweet the hours I passed away,*
> *With the girl I left behind me.*

I guess it took me a month or more, but I got it all dug out, and there was a wooden ladder and the walls were tarred cement blocks and there was a hatch and a padlock and nobody could hear me when I was down there, not even when I shouted and screamed and pounded on the wooden hatch, and nobody could hear my father either, trapped in that white room of madness, nobody could hear him even though he screamed until the veins in his neck bulged, and I'd made a whispered promise to get him out of the Castle just as soon as I could, and I aimed to keep that promise, yes I did.

*   *   *

In spite of everything, I was thinking that maybe salvation was in reach after all, even considering the naysayers and cynics who had condemned me, who had given up on me (a lad of only sixteen years!). And as far as the man who'd made the threats to my Constance, well, I wasn't going to let him bully her, and I certainly wasn't going to let him bully me. Think about what the Soldier would do, he certainly wouldn't let a beautiful woman like Constance be brutalized. I would have to find some way to stop it.

And so I waited until she was gone, until they were both gone, and I went to the rear of her cabin and smashed the window with a crowbar and climbed in, and there was shattered glass everywhere and my hands and body got all bloody, but I laughed at pain, always had.

Well, it was strange and more than a little exciting to be inside Constance's home, and I explored for a while, spending quite some time in each room. Kitchen: kerosene stove, white porcelain sink with dirty dishes piled high, small black metal table and black metal chairs, linoleum rug, Kelvinator refrigerator, nearly empty. Bathroom: pull-chain toilet, claw-foot bathtub, medicine cabinet filled with toothbrush, Paxil, Buspirone, skin cream, Luvox. Living room:

fireplace, floral couch, Persian rug, television, CD player with sad Beethoven inside.

No signs of the psychotic ex-husband, but he'd been around, he'd made his presence known, poisoning her mind with lies, and inside the bedroom it was all filled with melancholy and depression, the blankets pulled into a heap at the bottom of the bed, clothes strewn all over the place, romance novels on the nightstand. And the most surprising thing, in the corner of the room, a crib, blankets neatly made, a mobile dangling, and that was who she'd lost, her baby, her boy, her Benton, a picture in a locket, no wonder she was so sad, no wonder her eyes had been crying forever.

I lay in bed and drank some of the gin I'd taken from the kitchen and I had my Browning knife and I just waited and waited and I was the Soldier and I was wearing a gas mask, and they'd made Constance wear a mask, and they were doing terrible things to her, taking their turns on her, and there were plenty of guards with primitive AK-47s, and everybody told me that it was too dangerous, that these guards would take care of me, but I sneaked up behind them and slit their throats and there was blood everywhere, and I grabbed Constance and her legs didn't work, so I slung her over my shoulder and we disappeared into the mountains and into the caves and eventually we were at the Skull Shack, and I nursed her to health and she gave herself to me, and now her bed was filled with holes that I'd made with my Browning knife.

And then I heard a sound at the door and I panicked and then the front door opened and she was humming a song I'd never heard. I guess you could say adrenaline set in, and I was the Soldier again. Well, I tried yanking the bedroom window open, but it wouldn't budge, and I could hear her whistling in the living room. Then I pulled again and this time it opened, but not all the way, and it also made a creaking sound, and I heard Constance say, hello? Is anyone there? And there I was, halfway in and halfway out, and I must have looked ridiculous, and panic rose through my body, and I pushed and pushed, and eventually I tumbled to the ground below. And not ten seconds later, Constance opened the bedroom door and walked toward the window, but I was pressed against the wall where she couldn't see me, and she stood there for a long time, and I'll bet she was just as scared as could be, and then after a while I heard her voice again, only now she was on the phone with the police saying there's somebody been in my house, and I felt just like Goldilocks, only I wouldn't escape scot-free, no way José, they knew it was me, they knew it was me the whole time, and they gave me probation, and I was thankful for that, and they gave me a restraining order, and I was mad as hell about that, because it wasn't Constance who wanted it, it was that possessive ex-husband of hers, and I decided right then and there that I would have to rescue her from him and take her to a place where she couldn't be tortured anymore, and I had the perfect place, and you know where that is.

CHAPTER 21

Oh, those next few weeks were cold, colder than a silver miner's ass as they say, and it was snowy too, with sheets and sheets falling over the mountain until everything looked like a massive heap of marshmallows, and my uncle and aunt were so angry with me about what had happened with Constance, about the breaking and entering and the meeting with the judge and all the rest, but they only knew one side of the story and it pained me not to be able to tell them the TRUTH about her controlling ex-husband, and the TRUTH about her dead baby, and the TRUTH about her passion for me, but you always worry about people's reactions, so I kept my mouth shut.

And once I made the mistake of asking them about my father and whether I could go visit him in the Castle. Oh, it will be a long time before you see him again, they said, and you could just tell they were enjoying it, and then a thought came to me, maybe they benefitted from his incarceration, maybe they got all the money that he had hidden under the floorboards, well, there was certainly a lot of that!

So one morning when my thoughts were clear, and the voices in my skull were only whispers, I decided that I wouldn't be following their rules anymore, in fact, I wouldn't be following anybody's rules anymore, because I'd spent my whole life following rules, and look at where it had gotten me. And maybe the rule-makers could prevent me from seeing Constance, but they couldn't prevent me from seeing my own father now could they? So I made some plans...

*   *   *

Some days later: me trudging through the snow wearing an orange pom-pom hat, a ragged jacket and worn-out boots, my ears and nose and fingers and toes numb, the Castle far away. I can tell you that I never wished for a car more than on this particular afternoon, a good car with a hemi and studded tires and heat blasting through the vents. You never get used to the cold, and I was discouraged and sobbing quietly. But whenever I felt like giving up and turning around, I thought about the Soldier and the way he would have responded, and he wouldn't have let a little snow and cold get in his way, so I marched on.

A couple of miles down the road, God said hey Benton let me give you a break, poor guy, and he got a semi to stop before the snow started dumping again. The driver was a friendly little guy with slicked-back straw hair, a Fu Manchu mustache, and glasses that got lighter and darker and lighter again. Where are you heading, he asked me, and I told him Denver, and then I told him the story of how they'd dragged my father away against his will when he hadn't done anything wrong except for love his wife, and Fu Manchu raised his eyebrows and said, that's some heavy shit, son, and I couldn't argue with him on that count.

This is interesting: I'd never been off the Mountain in my whole life. Well, my father used to say Silverville is a little piece of heaven here on Earth, a place of natural beauty where people mind their own business. You leave the Mountain and that's when people start asking questions, that's when people start pushing you around and dragging you down. That's where they judge you by your clothes and your friends and your skin. Not on the Mountain, he said. People leave you alone there.

But Father was wrong as you can clearly see.

Fu Manchu drove fast, down, down, down, and soon we were off the Mountain. And then rumbling down the highway toward the buildings, the noise, the world; the knee-high snow now a memory with no meaning.

And my driver had taken me just as far as he could take me, and I didn't know where the Castle was, not exactly, so he dropped me off on a street lined with bail bonds and liquor stores and crumbling buildings and black people, said good luck, son, hope you find your father, son, hope you find some peace, son.

I wandered down the street, looking up and down and all around, and strange-looking creatures gnawed at my heels and asked me for money, asked me what I wanted, asked me what I was doing here. I had twenty-four dollars that I'd borrowed from Aunt Rose's purse, and I was feeling some pangs of hunger, so I stopped in a little Chinese restaurant, and they shouted at me in English, but it wasn't an English I had ever heard before, and the menu was a plastic book and I pointed at words that I recognized and five minutes later a Chinaman slid a plate of chicken and rice in front of me.

I scarfed that food down lickety-split; then I paid and asked the Chinaman how to get to the Castle and he spoke to me in that strange English again, and he sure seemed mad at me, so I left and started walking down Colfax Avenue and I saw a tattoo parlor and I figured that it sure would be something to get a tattoo, maybe of the Soldier aiming his rifle, but I didn't have enough money so instead I went inside and asked a man with tattoos crawling up his neck if he knew where the Castle was, that my father was a patient there, and he looked at me like I was crazy, said he'd never heard of it, so I left there too and kept walking and talking and walking some more.

I wandered the streets for hours on end, searching for the Castle, asking around, getting no leads. And then finally when I'd just about given up all hope, when I'd resigned myself to never seeing my flesh and blood again, I saw this old black man rubbing his hands over a trash can bonfire, and I had a feeling about him, and sure enough he knew exactly what I was talking about. Sure I know the Castle, he said. My only daughter spent some time there. Only it's called Colorado Psychiatric Hospital now. It ain't too far from here…

And it wasn't far, he was right about that. Two miles, maybe less. The location of the building was kinda strange. What I mean by that was the neighborhood, how it was surrounded by blocks and blocks of single-family residences, sad little ranches, and then all of a sudden this big brick building, and it didn't look anything the way I expected, in fact it looked just like any other building, and I decided that was a pretty good metaphor, how crazy people look like everybody else, sometimes it's hard to pick them out of a lineup, if you know what I mean.

Well, the sun was setting over the mountains, dropping faster than you might think. I took off my hat and gloves and combed my hair with my fingers, and it occurred to me that I hadn't looked in a mirror in some weeks, and I walked toward the front door, and my shadow was long and crooked and it was howling even though I was quiet.

The inside of the hospital wasn't anything, and I couldn't hear any screaming, which I guess surprised me. There was a woman behind the counter and her hair was black and her clothes were white and her smile scared me something terrible. May I help you, she said, but the way she said it, I knew she didn't really want to help me, nobody really wanted to help me.

I'm looking for my dad, I said, and there was a momentary glimmer of pity in her parakeet green eyes, but that disappeared quickly and then it was the usual meanness that I'd been noticing lately. Who's your dad, she said and I told her his name. She tapped on a keyboard for a few moments, and I could see the glow of the monitor reflecting in her glasses.

Corrosion

Ah yes, she said, and then she typed some more
and I waited for her to let me in on the secret. After
a couple of minutes she said: Flan Faulk. He's under
the care of Dr. Polson. Right now the visitor policy is
restrictive.
What does that mean? I asked.
It means your father can't have visitors. Not even
you.
Oh, and there was glee and vindication in this
devil nurse's voice! I asked for more information:
Why couldn't he have any visitors? What was the
treatment plan? Because I'd heard about lobotomies,
knew the drill. Lift the eyelid and place the icepick
against the top of the eye socket, pound through with
a mallet...
Well, the nurse couldn't give me any answers,
couldn't help me one bit, so I let slip a vulgar com-
ment about the size of her ass, and she said that I
needed to kindly remove myself from the premises,
and if I didn't go willingly, security would be summoned. It didn't take long for me to realize I had
made a mistake, and I became emotional, apologizing and apologizing, saying I don't know what the
fuck got into me, I've been under pressure, so much
goddamn pressure. But the nurse wasn't impressed
and her eyes narrowed to slits and with a certain
amount of contempt she said, the sins of the father
are the sins of the son. Then she grinned, baring inci-
sors all coated with blood and plaque.
I felt a wave of anger, a slow-burning rage that
started in my face and traveled all the way through
my body; I was about to lose control again, and this
time with fireworks! The nurse picked up the phone

and I slapped it out of her hand. Then, with the Soldier leading the charge, I leapt over the secretary's desk and made a dash for the corridor...

CHAPTER 22

And then I was barreling down the hallway, past doctors and orderlies, past walls of brick and floors of linoleum, witnessing a parade of the maimed and insane flashing before my eyes at warp speed: a young man, quiet and obedient, left hand flexed into a claw, right hand flapping uselessly at his side; a woman, twenty or forty or sixty, face wide and short, head balding, eyes venomous, mouth spitting and cursing and shrieking; a gentle-looking fellow with a sweater-vest and an Irish accent, acting as a watchman, neck strained forward, head turning slowly back and forth, peering down the hallway; a woman with a bone jutting from the center of her forehead, believing herself to be the Virgin Mary; a man with thinning red hair and a bent nail in his mouth, talking about a recent murder (I hit him on the back with a piece of wood. So nicely was it done that not a

Jon Bassoff

drop of blood was spilled. I only laid him to sleep.);
a grotesque man or woman, twitching terribly, eyes
wild and bloodshot, mouth covered by a respirator
mask; an elderly woman, recently transferred from
the House of the Aged and Infirm, in a state of terror
about a man upstairs planning to shoot her to death;
a Mexican calling himself El Presidento running the
hallway completely nude, claiming to be tainted
with syphilis and the yellow fever, corneas opaque
and encrusted with blood vessels...

And soon they were all after me, the employees
and sick alike, a George Romero production, while
I ran and slid down the linoleum floor, pounding on
doors, calling out my father's name. But the corridor
went on forever, and electroconvulsive shock treatment was in vogue, and then I saw the rats crawling
out from beneath a particular doorway and I knew
he was in there, and I was shouting Dad...Dad...
Dad, but it was no use, it was never any use, and they
soon caught me and tied me to a gurney and shot
me full of medicine, and I said to the nurse any idea
when I'll be able to see him, I'm lost without him,
and she shook her head and said she would be more
than happy to contact me when the time was right,
and I thanked her a million and left and there had
been no shouting or cursing, no calls to security, no
sprints down the corridor.

* * *

That night I stayed in a little motel and it was
called the Lamplighter and they had termites and
bad plumbing and towels with lipstick smudges and

a swimming pool painted black so they'd never have to clean it. I called my aunt and uncle, told them I was safe, told them I'd gone on a little trip, nothing to worry about, and I could tell they were relieved, they weren't bad people, if only there were more people like them, I thought, and then I closed the blinds and locked the door, and I slept well, like an anesthetized log as they say, didn't have dreams of madhouses and lobotomies, did have dreams of the Soldier and Constance, my beautiful Constance, woke up sad and wishing that the world was maybe prettier a little bit.

Used the last of my borrowed money to buy a breakfast burrito with black beans and chicken and pepper jack cheese, then got lucky again and hitch-hiked partway up the mountain with an elevator salesman who'd been married to the same woman for twenty-eight years, and not once had she been true to him, he finding matchbooks in her purse from every bar and motel in Denver, he wondering how she'd gotten pregnant when he'd had a vasectomy at eighteen years old!

And finally home after a long hike, relieved in a way, Aunt Rose loving on me more than ever before, hugging me and kissing me, saying we were so worried about you, sweet Benton! She made me macaroni and cheese smothered in ketchup (yum my favorite) and even Uncle Horace was kind, saying I could talk to them about anything, do you understand, anything, that I didn't have to worry about them being disappointed in me, etcetera, etcetera. What it really came down to, of course, was that they wanted me to spill the beans about my little field trip, they wanted me to tell them where I'd been. But despite their assurances of unconditional love, I wasn't about to let them know that I'd been in search for my father, because then they would have made me see some Dr. Sigmund (don't deny it, it's a fact) who would have made me talk about my insecurities and neuroses and Oedipus fantasies and all the rest of that crap, would have pried into the deep recesses of my mind through therapy or hypnosis or torture, probably the latter.

So I went to sleep that night with a packed belly and clarity of thoughts, knowing full well that tomorrow everything would change, that maybe some people would fall to their knees begging for mercy, begging for reconsideration.

*   *   *

Uncle Horace owned a Winchester 1200 shotgun and it was for self-protection. He kept it on the top shelf of his closet but it wasn't a secret or anything, because he'd shown it to me before and shown me how to load it and all of that stuff. I'd never fired a gun, not even hunting, but I figured it wouldn't be very difficult, just load the shells into the magazine, pump them into the chamber, and squeeze the trigger to fire. Not that I'd need to shoot it, I only needed it because I was slight in frame and lacked the instant authoritarian standing that a Winchester did.

And so when Horace and Rose were gone at work and I was supposed to be back at school, I went into the closet and borrowed that shotgun and several rounds, and then I went outside to the shed and sawed it off nice and short with a hacksaw. It fit okay underneath my jacket, which was good because I didn't want to scare Constance, not right away anyway.

It had started snowing again, and I was glad about that, because my feet were quiet when I walked, and I wasn't worried about footprints because I'd never worn these boots before and I'd get rid of them as soon as I was done—I had thought about most everything. And I imagined that I was The Soldier, and I was talking to the rest of my platoon, telling them Godspeed and all the rest of that crap, but then I figured I'd better stop talking out loud in case anybody was listening, so I had those conversations in my head.

And I knew Constance's schedule, knew she wouldn't be getting home for another hour at least, but I wanted to make sure I was positioned properly in plenty of time because, as they say, to win a war quickly takes long preparation. I huddled behind a tree, the same lodgepole I'd always huddled behind, and the snow was falling and the sky was the color of lead.

You sing songs, ancient lullabies, and you tell yourself bedtime stories, the same ones your mother used to tell you, the one about the parents who leave their children in the woods hoping that the wild animals will get them, and you wait for your Love to make an appearance with that garland of flowers in her hair and lips all blood-red and mascara dribbling down her cheeks...

Time passed slowly, seconds taking hours, and then she was there, different than I expected, no flowers in her hair. She walked slowly to the side of the cabin and grabbed an armful of wood, a hardy woman. I could hear myself breathing and it was getting louder and louder and I worried that she might hear too, so I pinched my lips tight and stopped breathing for a time. And how I longed to lay my head on her chest, how I longed to feel the softness of her skin, how I longed to taste her sweat, taste her tears. She opened the screen door and lost her grip on the firewood and it came crashing to the ground, and then I could hear her mumbling and cursing. She didn't know, probably, that she was being watched; she didn't know, probably, that the big bad wolf was camouflaged nicely into the snow. After a while she got all the wood gathered up again and managed to get inside, allowing the screen door to slam shut behind her.

I waited and then I waited some more. The music from inside started playing, that Beethoven piano, all muted and hazy. The sky was turning black, the wind was blowing hard, and the world was a Christmas snow globe. My hands were buried deep in my carpenter jeans and my hat was pulled on tight, but my teeth wouldn't stop chattering. I knew the things I needed to do.

And suddenly a preacher shouting: You will hear the moaning, the cries of anguish. You will feel the skin peeling from your body. You will smell burning hair and flesh. You will taste the blood and bile. You will see a world in flames, a landscape of filth, and you will say give me one more chance, Lord, one more chance to be redeemed. And the Lord will say, You fool! I sacrificed my only son to free you, offered you a place in the House of the Lord, and you spat in my face, you pissed on my shoe. And now you come begging for redemption, for everlasting pleasure? The Lord is generous, but only to those who have served. You sinners, you whores, you shall get what is coming to you and then some!

Move forward: smoke was billowing from the chimney and the windows were dull orange and the air was shivering and a wounded coyote was shrieking and the ground was knee deep with icicles and the cabin was ready to explode and I was ready to explode and the door was open and I was standing there and I was holding the shotgun and Constance was screaming, tears welling in her eyes.

CHAPTER 23

Where is he? I shouted, and then I felt bad, shouting, holding a shotgun, so I calmed down a bit. I lowered the weapon, but she was still in a panic, still shaking and crying. I'm not gonna hurt you, I said. Understand me? I'm not gonna hurt you. I love you. But that sounded so ridiculous, pledging my love to her here, now, that I shook my head, started laughing all uneasy like.

What do you want? she said, her voice barely louder than a whisper. What are you going to do to me?

You don't have to be scared, I said. He's not gonna hurt you anymore. He's the one, isn't he? He's the one who killed your baby. He's the one who made you get that restraining order.

No answer.

It wasn't you. It couldn't have been you.

Please, she said. Just go away. I won't tell any-body that you've been here. Nobody needs to know.

But I just shook my head. I'm not leaving without you. I can't face myself without you anymore. Maybe you can understand that, maybe you can't. It doesn't matter. I know a place. It's up yonder a ways. No-body will ever find us there. We can be happy, may-be. It's worth a shot, maybe.

By this point I had entered her cabin and shut the door behind me, and I was raising the shotgun every once in a while, waving it around a bit, but it was out of nervousness, not meanness.

Her lower lip was trembling, and her cheek kept twitching, and she said, why me? What do you want with me? You're a nice-looking boy. Why don't you try to find somebody at school, somebody your own age? Why, I'm old enough to be your mother.

And just as soon as she said that, she knew she'd made a mistake, what with the fact that my mother was dead and all, and she tried apologizing, and I said, don't worry about it, no offense taken, and as far as questioning my judgment in my choosing you to be my bride, well the choice was never mine to make.

*   *   *

We left late that night and Constance had calmed down somewhat, that is she wasn't crying and screaming, not nearly as much anyway, but she still didn't want to go with me, kept begging me to re-lease her, said she knew that I was in pain, said that there were people out there who could help me, and I realized just how badly this man, this mountain, had poisoned her thinking.

The sky was the color of coal, and the stars and the moon shone dully, giving us just enough light to see a couple feet in front of us, but I could have led us blindfolded, that's how well I knew these mountains. And I kept that shotgun pressed into the small of Constance's back, and I tried making conversation, talking about politics and religion and such, but she wanted no part of it, so I took to singing old '60s country songs, songs my father used to play on his Lenco turntable: George Jones and Marty Robbins and Don Gibson. D Key: *The lights in the harbor don't shine for me. I'm like a lost ship adrift on the sea – sea of heartbreak.*

Well, eventually she started talking to me, maybe because she didn't like my singing voice, maybe because she was scared of the dark. She asked me questions, questions about my father, questions about my mother. What was she like? She had long black hair. She was a terrible cook. She loved me some of the time. She loved my father less than that. What did she die of? Sickness. She died of sickness. My father…he kept her body. Even after she died. He didn't want to let her go. You can't blame him for that. Life is too brutish and mean. You can't blame my father. They took him away for loving her…

Late at night in the mountains, you start seeing strange things. A man hanging from a lodgepole, eyes bugging out from his skull, tongue lolling from his mouth; a coyote gnawing on its own wounded leg, blood spreading across the mountain floor; a woman in a white nightgown, waist deep in a river, rocking a dead baby to sleep; a miner from long ago, pickaxe in one hand, Carbide lamp in the other...

And here's the truth: I wasn't scared but she was, she was very scared, and not just of the ghost miner, she was scared of the mountain, she was scared of me. She asked me questions, but I didn't ask her any because I knew her story, I'd always known her story. And then an icy wind blew across the mountain, through the skeleton trees, and death was spinning wildly through the air, and I knew that Constance wouldn't be long for this world, maybe. And I knew that I wouldn't be long for this world, certainly.

We made it to the Skull Shack and nobody would find us there. It was cold inside so I started working on making a fire, but I watched her from the corner of my eye, making sure she didn't lunge for the shotgun, making sure she didn't lunge for the door, but she didn't, she was acting like a dog that's been kicked for pissing on the carpet, all huddled up against the wall.

And it took me a long time to get the fire going because the wood was wet, and I started getting good and frustrated, and even though Constance wasn't smiling, I could tell that she was enjoying every minute, watching me struggle, and I felt the urge to hurt her, but I didn't, I would never hurt her, probably, I was here to protect her from the world, from this putrid, rotting, decomposing cunt of a world, and I told her, I'll never hurt you, you've got to believe me, I'll never hurt you, just don't try escaping, this world should be strangled and beaten and left for dead.

So we got married and it was a quiet affair with no family and no wedding cake and there she was lying in the fetus position, shoulders heaving up and down, red hair strewn everywhere, blood trickling from her nose, eye swollen and purple-like. And that's the way it went for a long time, us married, but her not happy about it. We had plenty of food and plenty of drink, in fact, we had everything we would ever need. And I was sure that her restlessness would fade after a while, just as soon as she learned a thing or two about love and loyalty, but in the meantime it was a battle to stay awake. I just knew that if I fell asleep first, fell asleep at all, she would sneak out of the cabin with a pitter-pat, pitter-pat, and I'd be alone and more hateful than ever, so I stayed awake, maybe drifting off for a second here or there, but I'd always jerk awake with a coating of blood on my eyes, and she watched me, planning, planning.

I needed sleep, needed to do something. Eventually, I tried one of those cowbells around her neck. At first she thought it was real funny, saying that's a crazy idea, Benton, but once the thing was bolted on, she saw that I was serious and she didn't smile about it no more. Just know, I wasn't meaning to be cruel, but it was getting to be awful hard to stay awake night after night after night after night, and now every time she'd get up to piss or get a drink of water, I'd hear that ringing and I'd open one eye and say, don't go running off, you hear, and she didn't, she didn't dare.

Well, it's hard to know how many days and nights we spent at the Skull Shack, but I started drinking more and more, that cheap plum brandy, and when I got good and drunk, I became mean, and I wasn't proud of it, and then sometimes I'd cry and cry like a little baby, ask Constance: you know what it's like always being an outcast, you know what it's like always having people whisper behind their hands, saying that boy's not right, that whole family's not right? and sometimes she would just watch me like my father watching the rats, and sometimes the humanity would seep from her pores and she'd stroke my head and say don't cry, it's a lousy world, don't cry, Benton.

* * *

And back at home, Aunt Rose and Uncle Horace sat at the kitchen table looking grave, staring out the porthole window at the ink-black trees, singing: *Oh where you have you gone, Billy Boy, Billy Boy? Oh, where you gone, Charming Billy?* And they called the local sheriff, and the sheriff pushed up the brim of his Stetson hat and shook his head and spat, said, we'll keep our eyes open, yes we will, but when a kid his age has the mind to up and run away, there ain't much we can do.

But I knew they'd come looking, sure as shit that. How long could we hide? Not forever, not even close. Please take this bell off my neck, she said. I'm not gonna run.

And her eyes were wide and soft and truthful so I believed her.

And she lied.

CHAPTER 24

Not much of a plan really, just wait until I fall asleep, swipe my gun and leave. She didn't have the heart or guts to shoot me in the temple while I slept, and I was only mildly thankful for that because death comes in many forms, not just when you stop breathing.

Back outside and the weather was as nasty as it gets with the wind howling and the snow falling and I knew Constance couldn't get far in this type of weather, knew that she didn't know the mountains the way I did, but having her freeze to death in some snowdrift wouldn't do me any good, so I looked and looked and I called out her name, and my voice sounded strange, didn't sound like my own really, as if my body had been taken over by something troubling and terrible that I couldn't name.

Corrosion

I had my lantern and the snow was knee deep and I looked for footprints, looked for breadcrumbs, but there were just endless layers of snow, a heavenly light illuminating the white plain, in every direction white lines of falling snow, and time didn't exist anymore and Constance was out there somewhere, barreling down the mountain, or huddled beneath a tree, and I needed to find her. I stopped where I was and closed my eyes. And then the Soldier was standing before me with a gas mask wrapped tightly across his face, and he took me by the hand and we walked and I begged him to show me his face and he shook his head and we walked some more and the wind was angrier than ever and I was blind, but the Soldier led me.

Everywhere everything was white and when I looked at the sky, I could see the darkness, but then the darkness vanished and all I saw was the snow, and the sky was bright everywhere and the wind kept changing directions and the Soldier had his head down and he kept walking, not seeming to notice or care about the blowing snow. And I could hear the crunching of our boots and my feet were growing numb and I couldn't stop shivering and then I saw Constance up ahead, barely visible through the mist, and she was stumbling through the drifts, the shotgun dangling from her hand.

Then the Soldier left and I called out her name and she turned to face me, gun pointed in my direction. She shouted for me to stop but I kept walking because I didn't care anymore, and she cocked the weapon and warned me again, but I kept walking forward. It was a miracle, praise God, that I'd found her, and I knew some things were meant to be. When I was within ten or so yards of her, she squeezed the trigger and there was a deafening noise and I was on the ground and now the horizon wasn't just white anymore, and she'd grazed my left arm, but I felt no pain despite the blood that was making the snow dirty.

Constance stood over me, and her face had changed, it had become that of the devil, with blood and scars and bruises all over it. She raised the shotgun again, but this time I was ready. I rolled out of the way and she fired and missed and I grabbed at her legs and got just a piece, and she fell into the snow and the shotgun fell from her hands.

One arm wasn't working but I didn't need it, I snatched the gun from the snow and got on top of her and pushed the barrel against her neck, and she fought, but her effort was halfhearted because she knew it was over, and I could have killed her, but I loved her, you've got to understand me, so I stopped, and she was choking and gasping for breath. Mustering all the strength I could manage, I lifted her and slung her over my shoulder, and she was almost a corpse, my father loved that woman with all of his might, that's why he refused to let her go, what's the crime in that?

Back up the mountain, shotgun over one shoulder, bride over the other. And now, forever, snow falling, wind howling, boots crunching, breath wheezing, devil laughing.

*   *   *

Corrosion

I made a tourniquet out of my T-shirt, wrapped it around my arm, and lit a fire, watching Constance as she sat in the corner of the Skull Shack, crying and crying, like it was she who'd been shot. And I felt some pity, but not too much, and one thing was clear: she wasn't going to stay in the shack of her own volition, she'd leave the first chance she got, and wasn't no cowbell gonna do the job nowadays.

She sat in the corner of the shack and she barely looked human, what with the way her face was all bruised and bloody and filthy, her hair all matted and wild. She watched with interest as I walked across the shack and removed an old piece of carpet. Sad and angry, I unlocked the padlock and slammed open the hatch door to the root cellar, motes of dust filling the air. Ugly thoughts taunting me. With some confidence, but not much, I grabbed the shotgun from next to the fireplace and said I didn't aim to hurt her, told her to get on up and come with me. But she didn't move, didn't say a word, just stared at me, her body trembling like winter.

Gonna need you to go down to the cellar, I said, just can't afford for you to go running off again. Know that I aim to feed you and take good care of you. No reaction. So I cocked the shotgun and aimed it at her head, but she didn't budge even a little bit, calling my bluff, knowing I loved her too much to harm her.

And that's the way it was for some time, me pointing the gun at her, and her just staring at me, staring right through me, if you want to know the truth of it. Gonna need you to go down to the cellar, I said again, and this time I took a few steps toward her. Her face got all worried-looking and she shrieked, and I raised the butt of the shotgun high into the air and came down hard onto her head. She melted onto the floor, and for a second I was afraid I'd hit her too hard and killed her maybe, but after a few moments I saw her move and heard her groan, so I knew she was alive, at least for the time being.

No turning back, I grabbed her by the feet and dragged her slowly across the floor, toward the cellar. The fire was burning and I felt warm and thankful to be alive, and I missed my mother more than anything, and I missed my father more than anything, and I wasn't going to lose anybody else, not without a fight, not without a fight.

Her mouth was sort of bobbing open and shut, and she was mumbling something, nonsense all. And then we got to the cellar opening and I grabbed her beneath the arms and carried her down the wooden ladder toward the darkness, the great darkness where she'd stay.

And there was a cot with blankets and a pillow, and suddenly I felt very sad, knowing that nothing lasts forever, not even the wind or hills or rain, and I kissed her on her lips, and her eyelids fluttered open, and her eyes darted back and forth across her skull like fingerlings.

I started climbing back up the ladder, saying, I'll see you soon, my love, my heart, my forever. I pulled myself out of the dugout and started to close the hatch, and then Constance pulled herself to her knees and, in a little girl's voice, said, don't leave me this way. Please. Don't leave me this way. I stared down at her and she was just a shadow, I stared down at her and she was just my mother, I stared down at her and whispered I'm sorry. I closed the door and secured the padlock.

CHAPTER 25

Just like when I returned from my adventure to the Castle, Aunt Rose and Uncle Horace were happy to see me, I could tell, saying we've been worried sick about you, we thought something terrible, absolutely terrible had happened to you, and I clicked my heels and said no place like home, and I ate a meal of trout fishcakes and elk jerky, and they asked me all sorts of questions, about my whereabouts, about my wounded arm, but I just shook my head and said I didn't much want to talk about it, that all's well that ends well, and they didn't press me further although they glanced at each other with anxious looks on their faces.

I slept well that night, didn't think about Constance hardly at all. Soon, I would go and visit her, make sure she had food and drink, make sure she was comfortable, she couldn't escape from there, you couldn't blame my father, he tried his best to save her, it was the Christ Rat that failed. Do you remember how Moses led his people across the desert but couldn't enter Israel? That was a cruel trick by God, that's the kind of guy he is sometimes, playing practical jokes for his own amusement, but it's not funny when people are drowning in tsunamis, when people are burning in fires, when people are freezing in blizzards. I heard about a guy once, and he was a good guy, and he had a wound on his elbow, and he didn't think much of it, but it started getting infected, and he got a fever of 104, and he went to the hospital, and they said holy shit you've got this and this, and it wasn't 24 hours later that the bacteria had eaten through all of his flesh and he'd lost both his arms and shoulders and all the skin on his torso, and what do you say to him, God, do you say I was just playing, isn't that a funny joke, well is that what you say, God, well is it, well is it?

But life was certainly looking up for me. Aunt Rose and Uncle Horace were being awfully nice to me, and there was no school on account of Christmas vacation, and everywhere you looked there was Christmas cheer, lights shining, tinsel twinkling, people saying, have you been a good boy, Benton, are you going to get a new train set, or is coal in store for you? And I would wink and say, depends on how closely Santa's been watching!

Every day or two I hiked up the mountain toward the tundra, toward the Skull Shack, where my wife waited without a care in the world. But Constance wasn't grateful for anything, you know the way women are. She drank the water and she ate the food, but there were no thank yous, there were no I love yous, there were no how are you, Bentons.

It's difficult to hear the whispers in the mountains, the wind blows too hard. But I could hear a goddamn pine needle dropping in the snow, blessed as I was with supernatural hearing, so I could sure as hell hear the whispers from my room, even though my door was closed, even though the wind was blowing. Aunt Rose and Uncle Horace saying that is very concerning, saying the boy couldn't have had anything to do with it, he's been with us the whole time, he's really turned a corner, he hasn't talked about her in such a long time. The mountain sheriff saying, I sure wouldn't mind talking to the boy. I'm sure he's not involved, but it would be good just to talk to him, just to find out what he knows. People do go missing in the mountains, usually by their own volition. But I sure would like to talk to the boy, if you don't mind.

Well, let me tell you about this mountain sheriff. I didn't trust him, didn't like him, despite his easygoing nature and comforting smile. He had a mustache, the type of mustache that I associate with child molesters, and he talked like a child molester, too, all nasally and overly friendly. Just want to find out if you've seen your friend Constance Durban at all in the past several days.

No, sir, I haven't. I have a restraining order, in case you don't remember. Can't be within 1,000 feet of her. It was her ex-husband who convinced her. Felt threatened by me. Can you imagine that? Threatened by a sixteen-year-old kid? How do you like that?

He smiled again. Now come on, Benton, he said. There's no ex-husband. You know that. Keeping the

Corrosion

pressure on. Trying to catch me in a lie, trying to catch me in an inconsistency. Well, Mr. Mountain Sheriff, I wasn't going to falter.

I haven't seen her, I said again. I'd tell you if I had. My aunt and uncle were satisfied and they said, anything else, Sheriff?

It's just troublesome, he said. Woman complains about being followed, complains about being stalked. A couple of weeks later she disappears. It's troublesome, that's all. And then he smoothed down his child molester mustache and shook his head. Well, I don't want to take up any more of your time. If any of you think of anything that might help us find her, would you mind giving me a call? And he handed each of us a business card. Sheriff Jim Tyler.

Uncle Horace and Aunt Rose each shook his hand and said certainly we will, certainly we will, but I didn't do any such thing, no reason to kiss up to a devilish troll. And so he glared at me with those suspicious eyes, said, see you around, Benton, see you around.

You think you've got it all figured out? You don't know shit! You hear me? You don't know shit!

*   *   *

Two days later, I left the mountain town of Silverville for good, made my way back to the Skull Shack, and they threw me a farewell parade, all the miners and fur trappers and whores lined up on Gold Street with their American flags and noisemakers and wind-chapped faces. Children hoisted on shoulders, babies soothed with bourbon-dipped pacifiers, pretty girls whispering and giggling. From the top of the hill, I could hear the high school marching band play "Auld Lang Syne."

But there were some strange goings on in the mountain and there is a world outside of my head. A dervish of snow falling and falling, and somewhere in the morning light a bowed psaltery playing a single note, never-ending. A small brick chapel, appearing like a fever dream, and behind it a graveyard. And an old man leaning against a fence, watching while a woman wearing a ragged beaver-fur coat—his wife maybe—digs into the earth with a round-point shovel. I stopped walking, said what are you digging the grave up for, and he said, don't you know the undertaker was a lunatic? Yes, mister, we have some reliable information that he desecrated all these bodies buried here, fucked their eye sockets and so forth, and now we diggin' 'em up to make things right again. The dead oughta have some peace, don't you think?

Well, I didn't know what to say, so I kept right on walking and I wasn't sure if the undertaker was crazy or if this husband and wife here were crazy, and then I placed my hands on my ears and I screamed and screamed, trying to exorcise the demons and angels, and the old man and his wife both smiled at me, their faces ravaged and pale.

*   *   *

We stayed in the shack, me in the living area, Constance down below, and we had enough canned food and soda to live for a month at least. She wasn't well, she told me she wasn't well, and she begged me to call for help, but it was too late for that. I'm sorry, I said to her, tears streaming down my ruddy cheeks, I'm so sorry. But if they find out the things I've done, they'll tie me up and lock me up. And if they find out the things I want to do, they'll take me to the Castle, and there's no escaping from there...

But it wasn't just Constance who was ill. My own health was failing: headaches, bloody noses, peeling skin, uncontrollable shaking. Casualty of war. I wondered what the Soldier would do.

He had a woman, you know. Elizabeth was her name. She was captured by a band of terrorists, raped and mutilated. Well, the Soldier came looking for her, and he found her, but they stuck a knife to her throat, said give us the information we need, we'll spare her life. And he stood there for a long time, and you could tell he was torn, the choice was between country and woman, and he shook his head and said, do what you need to do, and they sliced her throat, and he got good and mad and took care of each and every one of those Iraqis, and when he left, his uniform and face were covered with blood and he shook his head and said, God help me, but I ain't no traitor.

* * *

The winter was a cold one, and the snow never stopped falling, and darkness came earlier and earlier until there seemed to be no light at all. And there were moments of happiness, moments when I convinced myself that everything was going to be okay, but those moments disappeared like tears in the darkness, and misery crept through a crack in the window and sat on his haunches in the corner of the cabin, glaring at me with grim satisfaction.

CHAPTER 26

A week or more later they came for me. Nighttime and I could see them marching up the hill, a group of men, some in uniform, some in overalls. The authorities and the townsfolk. Holding torches and rifles and baseball bats.

Well, Constance must have sensed their presence because she got excited, started shouting and pounding on the latch. They knew about me, but they couldn't know about Constance, so I unlocked the padlock, and my hands were shaking and my nose was bleeding, and I opened the hatch door, and Constance had climbed up the ladder, and she didn't look much like a human anymore, and I kicked her hard in the temple and she screamed, then went toppling down the ladder like a rag doll, and then she was on the floor of the cellar, and she wasn't moving and I didn't know if she were dead or alive, I didn't know if I were dead or alive, and I closed the hatch and locked it and covered it with the throw rug and a stack of wood, and then they were pounding on the door, saying, c'mon Benton, we know you're in there, but the door was jammed shut with another pile of wood.

I knew this could be the end for me, but I wasn't going down without a fight, see I had the Father and the Soldier and the Christ Rat on my side, the Holy Trinity, so I used the fire poker to shatter the back window, and then I pulled my body through, and the broken glass cut through my skin, and I could hear them at the front door, pounding with those axes and baseball bats, and then I was running across the mountain floor, and each breath was a terrified scream, and only I knew that every tree was a murdered corpse, forever frozen with gnarled limbs, only I knew that the sky was swirling with tortured spirits and fallen angels, only I knew that the dirt was readying to open up and swallow me into its maw, and where was that music coming from, that strange music, deathly doo-wop from the broken speakers of a transistor radio.

I raced across the side of the mountain, feet sliding in the snow, grabbing a hold of branches when I could. The sky was as black as death itself, the moon a sliver of bone. And from behind, ghostly voices echoing across the mountain, unearthly firelight flashing spastically across the terrain.

I knew the mountain well, but when the moon disappeared behind the clouds, it became too dark and I was disoriented, lost in the cold and the snow, afraid that my frost-covered remains would be found, burrowed at the base of a lodgepole.

And I could tell they were closing in, could hear their voices echoing across the mountain, saying, we know you're out here, Benton. Show yourself before you freeze to death. We don't aim to hurt you, Benton. We just want to make things right.

And moments turned into minutes, and minutes turned into hours, and I prayed to God with all of my might, and God showed some sympathy, revealed a hiding place, a hiding place where I couldn't be found. A tunnel, barely visible in the darkness, and from the back of the cavern, voices whispering lovingly for me to come join them, and I pulled my way through the narrow opening, and it was cold and dark, and I felt like a blind man, unable to see inches in front of my eyes.

But I knew that a safety awaited me, a temporary sanctuary from the motley crew on the side of the mountain, its members howling in anguish at having lost their prey. My body was aching, slashed badly from the broken glass, and every movement filled me with pain, and still I pressed forward, a soldier in desperate retreat from his enemy.

The tunnel went on forever and the voices from the world became muted and then vacant and I never wanted to hurt Constance but it was the only way, and my heart was filled with anguish and fear as I climbed deeper into the cave, and I realized that now I was an animal, and I growled, and then suddenly my eyes sharpened and I could see with perfect clarity, could see the sinkholes and the speleothems, could see the bats and the flatworms and the ghosts...

I crawled forward, and I figured I would never

turn back. I could smell the rot of my mother's body, could hear the screams of Constance's nightmares, could see the death mask of my own face.

And the men who were searching for me, the men who wished to do me harm, they were gone, all gone, and I'd rather be eaten by the worms than spend my days in the Castle, so I placed my head on the cold ground and closed my eyes and slept and woke and there were bats and there were screams, and they were my screams, and God spoke to me, said I am with you, I will never leave you, my child, and I cried, but the tears were acid and they burned my skin, peeled it right off, and then my head was nothing but a Halloween skull, lolling back and forth, back and forth.

And after a night of forever, morning came, and a streak of light from somewhere, and I pulled myself forward, a soldier badly wounded, and it wasn't long until I reached God's temple, a small asylum at the end of the cavern. There was water on the floor and strange-looking crystals growing from the ceiling and for a moment I thought I was dead, but then I felt the slashes on my body and the melancholy in my brain and I knew that I was still dragging my body and soul across this mean old world.

So what else was there to do but wait? See, I couldn't be sure that my executors weren't waiting outside the cave, hiding behind the trees or in a dug-out trench with their rifles and torches, and I was sure they'd burn me at the stake. I had no food, but I could drink the water from the filthy stream, and dysentery was the least of my concerns.

And there were voices coming from everywhere,

so I covered my ears with my hands and rocked back and forth and couldn't you see it coming full circle, my father being dragged off to the mad house and finally them coming for me. You don't understand the kind of things they will do to me! There is a certain Dr. Freeman who drives from town to town in his lobotomobile, and he uses an icepick, places it beneath your eyelids, pounds it in with a mallet. Haven't you seen all of his patients wandering across the country, zombie-like, cognitive-reasoning mutilated, souls bleeding on the linoleum? You want me to join them in that horror flick? Well, do you? This was certain: I had to keep my wits about me.

Weeks or more passed and I'd shrunken below 75 pounds for sure, face gaunt, eyes flickering back and forth across my sockets. Eating worms and my own flesh, using a black rock to scrape messages in the wall: I am because I am because I am.

And then, just like that, the voices vanished and I wondered if it might be safe to go outside. Where were the men who hunted me? Where was Dr. Freeman and his ice pick?

It was hard to tell the nighttime from the day, hard to tell sleep from wakefulness, hard to tell madness from enlightenment. And if I were to creep out of the cavern and face the world once again, I'd have to do it on my own. There would be no ravens to send from this here ark, no voice of God making promises a day too late.

And so with true grit I returned to the narrow tunnel, all filled with disease-soaked bats and ravenous rats and everything not-so-nice, and I crawled on my scab-covered belly, and everything smelled like mildew and the end of the world, and outside the Mountain was still there, and it never goes away does it?

CHAPTER 27

It was morning time and the snow had stopped falling and the sun was rising above the craggy mountain, saying how do you do, Benton, good to see you back among the living, pity that it ain't gonna be for long! I trudged through the snow, and sometimes it reached above my knees, and I kept alert for the Searchers, kept alert for the Lobotomist, but it was just me, not even a crow screeching.

My jacket was warm and so was my pom-pom hat, but my jeans were soaking wet and I couldn't stop shivering, teeth a broken metronome. For a few minutes I wished that I were dead but then I worried about hell and what it would bring, so I kept pushing through the snow, searching for a familiar tree or rock, searching for Hansel's breadcrumbs.

I wondered how Constance was doing all alone in that fruit cellar, and I had been all alone in the cave, don't you forget that, and I wondered if she were hearing voices, I wondered if her God was still alive. Something you should know, Constance moaned when we made love, and it wasn't a moan of pain it was a moan of pleasure, so for those who say I'm a monster, I say I'm not a monster, for those who say I'm a monster, I say you're the real monster!

And then down the mountain a bit, a clearing and a path, barely visible in the snow. I was wheezing and I felt dizzy and I suppose I was staggering a bit along that trail. I thanked God that the day was sunny and not as cold, and it wasn't long until I found the dirt road that took me down the mountain, and I knew that I had to be careful because you never knew when the sheriff and his friends would leap out of the woods, baring fangs, so I walked behind the trees, parallel to the road, listening for engines, hoping I might be able to thumb a ride somewhere, somewhere far away.

Midmorning and the sun was lifting upward when I heard the faint hum of a motor, and I stood out there in the middle of the road, hoping he might stop, but it was a big old Caddy, and a fellow in a cowboy hat laid on that horn and I had no choice but to dive back into the snowbank. My hands were numb, and I wished I had my bottle of plum brandy, but instead I settled for a pinch of snuff, and then I wiped the snow off my clothes and laughed out loud and kept right on walking down that winter mountain road.

And time passed, and for a long time there were no more automobiles barreling down the mountain, and I got to feeling lonely and tired, maybe more lonely and tired than I ever had been, and so I began singing a song, and it was a song I had never heard before, but it was a song that had existed forever: *From the darkness in the sea to the sunshine on the hill in the forest filled with trees my shadow has gone still* and my mother had once said that there were those rare moments in our lives where there was an opportunity for real change, where we could leave our battered souls by the side of the road and pick up a new one that hadn't been so badly mutilated, but we had to know when those moments were because once they're gone they're gone and then we're stuck with our old souls and that's just about when all hell can break loose...

So I guess I knew from the time I saw the yellow headlights appear around the bend, I guess I knew from the time the old Chevy pickup slowed down and groaned to a stop, I guess I knew from the time the passenger-side door flung open, I just *knew* that this here was one of those moments.

I got into the pickup and pulled the door shut behind me, and I said I sure do appreciate the ride and then I looked up and I almost felt sick because his face was a mess, all burned and deformed, and he stuck out his hand and I shook it, and he said his name was Joseph Downs and where are you heading, and I said I just need to get off the mountain, and he said are you running from something, and I said we're all running from something, aren't we?

Well, I was in luck because not only was he leaving the mountain, but he was driving clear on through to Ohio, where his folks were. Said he hadn't seen them in some time...

Jon Bassoff

And then we didn't talk for a while, and he turned on the radio, old-time jazz, and hell was on my mind, a vague threat, but it couldn't be worse than the piss-pot known as Earth, so I rested easy on that, and I watched out the window as the snow and the mines and the trees rushed by so fast.

And nobody knew where Constance was, nobody knew if she were alive or dead, and I was a person of interest, but there were no roadblocks, there were no sheriff cars with their lights flashing in time.

By the time we reached the bottom of the mountain, the sun was sinking and the sky was turning a mess of pastels. Joseph Downs turned off the radio and pulled out a cigarette and asked if I wanted one, and I said thankee much, and we both smoked, and I knew he was going to tell me his story, knew he was going to tell me about his face, knew this was a story I didn't want to hear.

Tells about being a Marine, about being stationed in Mosul. Tells about his convoy driving down this dirt road, trying to secure the area. Tells how it was pitch-black and their lights were off and they wore night goggles. Tells how they came to a bridge over a canal and how the bridge exploded and his eardrums exploded and the Humvee exploded. Tells about how there were flames everywhere and the insurgents had gotten them but good and he knew he was hurt bad but couldn't feel any pain. Tells about the detached legs and arms he witnessed, the decapitated heads. Tells about being pulled out by a soldier with a gas mask and then finding himself in a chopper, flying over the burning desert, not sure if he was dead or not, wishing he was.

189

Corrosion

And he told me this story over the course of an hour at least, and he cried and laughed while telling it, and I listened to every detail, memorized every detail, and it occurred to me that this guy was a real hero, and it's better to experience pain and heartache than to experience nothing at all...

They wouldn't let me see a mirror for some time, he said, and when they finally did, they had all sorts of doctors and orderlies and psychiatrists at my bedside. And I saw my face, and it wasn't a face that I recognized. I cried for a long time after that. You go to save the world. You don't figure that it's you that'll need saving.

They'd tried calling his parents but hadn't been able to get a hold of anybody. And when he found out that the hospital was trying to contact his next of kin, he got very angry. He didn't want anybody to know what had happened to him, didn't want people to see his face, didn't want people to see his soul. And the orderly, an Asian woman who smelled of lavender, promised that they wouldn't call again, not until he was ready.

Well, by this time Joseph Downs and I had both torn through a handful of cigarettes and I offered him some snuff but he didn't want any. Never cared for it, he said. And now the Mountain was in our rearview mirror, and so was the Skull Shack and the nightmares inside.

As he continued talking, I could feel strange sensations on my arms and legs, parasites crawling under my skin, and I knew that I'd contracted whatever disease my mother had had...

While in the hospital he'd been visited by a soldier in his brigade and this soldier said that he should consider himself lucky, that nearly everybody else in the Humvee had been killed. Well, that got him good and riled and he told the soldier that there were some things a hell of a lot worse than dying and those sons-of-bitches had it easy compared to him. And then he made the soldier an offer that he couldn't refuse. He gave him one of his dog tags. He instructed him to find his father in Ohio. Told him to give his father the dog tag. Tell him the story, just like it had happened. Only tell him that he'd died. And in exchange for this deception he offered the soldier $5,000.

Well, the soldier had done what he'd been told and so Joseph Downs was dead, another corpse in the desert, only now he wanted a resurrection, and don't we all?

CHAPTER 28

And it was all beginning to make sense now, my destiny was manifesting itself, and I had God to thank for that. And I remembered my father the scientist saying that God had decomposed and we must not weep for him. Well, my father was wrong. God was alive and well, but we couldn't understand his ways, not most of the time.

So what were you doing in the mountains? I asked Joseph Downs.

Hiding, he said. Nobody saw me; I saw nobody else. I was a ghost and nothing more.

But now he'd decided that he didn't want to be a ghost anymore, he decided that maybe life was worth living even without a human face. And now he was going to return to his childhood home and he wasn't sure how his father was going to react, didn't know if it would be joy or fury or both.

My own father had never been accepted by the scientific community, that's why he'd moved to the mountains. Oh, but he'd showed me some things, showed me the way chemicals reacted, and I couldn't help thinking of all the cans of Sterno he'd hoarded, just in case, Benton, just in case.

And when Joseph Downs was done talking about himself, about the war, about his death and rebirth, he started asking me some questions, out of curiosity, out of politeness, and I dreaded when people asked me questions. Questions about my past. Questions about my family. Questions about my future. I answered each and every inquiry with a lie, made up outlandish stories, and he glanced at me nervously from the corner of his eye, and I wondered just what he was thinking then.

Two hours of driving and eastern Colorado was the devil's land, nothing but sagebrush and dirt all dusted by the snow, the occasional farm, occasional car, occasional piss-pot town. The wind never stopped blowing, and don't you know the wind drove people crazy, caused normal men to slaughter their families and then sit in front of the television watching game shows with the volume up full blast until the police arrived.

And you see strange things out on the plains, and you wonder if the driver sees them too: an old woman on the roof of a shanty, spinning a weaving wheel; a dusty roadside billboard advertising *6 Gals For $1.00*; a grain elevator tilted like the Tower of Pisa; an auctioning of slaves in front of a textile mill; a destitute family lying facedown on the railroad tracks.

My Browning knife was in my front pocket, and

I knew I'd have to use it, but I'd never used it on another human, just our dog, after she broke her back, to put her out of her misery. Dad had put her in the wheelbarrow and made me push her out through the woods and I slit her throat and watched her twitch and die, and I cried for a long time, and my father helped me bury her, but my mother was sick in bed.

So you wonder if you can actually do it, start thinking that it's a hell of a thing killing a man, and then you remember that you've got God on your side, and you realize that Joseph Downs is The Soldier, and you realize that you're Joseph Downs.

Before the war, I had a girlfriend, he said. She's still in Ohio. Who knows, I might go knocking on her door. I think she'll scream in fright...

Joseph Downs laughed at the thought. And that's when I pulled out my knife. With one quick motion I jerked his head toward me with my left hand and sliced horizontally across his throat with my right. Blood started gushing from the hole in his throat, and he tried controlling the car, but it was no use, it careened off the highway and went rolling through a frost-covered field of nothing, eventually coming to stop in front an oversized wooden arrow pointing upward, reading *Prepare to Meet God*.

But Joseph Downs wasn't dead, not yet anyway. He was squeezing his neck, trying to hold in the life, but blood was seeping through his fingers, and he was staring at me with eyes of death, and I thought of Jesus, and I was still holding my blood-smeared knife.

And then he died and it was easy to tell when it happened because his shoulders slumped and his face relaxed and his eyes stopped blinking. I sat there for a long time and the wind stopped blowing and everything was quiet and still and he was squeezing his own throat; he had strangled himself to death.

*   *   *

I opened the door and stepped out of the car and looked around. There were miles and miles of loneliness and desolation and it was as good a place as any for Joseph Downs to die, and I vomited on the ground and wiped my mouth, and I knew what I had to do, but I was feeling unsteady and dizzy so I lay down on the ground and stared into the sky of gray and thought it sure is a funny world.

I might have fallen asleep, but not for long, because I heard the distant sound of an engine and I sat up and crawled behind the pickup, peered over the bed. It was a semi, but the driver didn't slow down, never noticed the wayward truck or the corpse inside, and even if he had, better to keep moving, better not to stick your nose into such disasters, benefits are minimal.

Once I'd gotten my bearings straightened out, I walked around to the other side of the truck and opened up the driver's-side door. It was harder work than you might think, but eventually I pulled the veteran's body from the truck and dragged it around back. I reached into his pockets for his wallet. I popped open the trunk, and then the wind started blowing again, and I pulled him up from under his arms, and I was sweating and breathing heavily, and then he was inside the trunk and I slammed it shut,

Corrosion

and the Mountain seemed like such a long time ago.

*   *   *

I sat in the pickup and looked through his wallet and I felt bad, like I was violating him, but then I remembered that he was dead as hell, and you couldn't violate a dead man. Inside the wallet there was a picture of a girl, and she had blonde hair and blue eyes and she was pretty enough, and she thought Joseph had died and now Joseph *had* died. There were no credit cards, but there was cash, close to five hundred dollars, and I knew that would get me started. And then I looked at his driver's license, and that caused me to lose my breath, because his face in the picture wasn't deformed, his face in the picture was handsome and proud, and he was ready to go to a foreign land and serve his country, save the world. The world hadn't been saved, his country hadn't been served, his body and soul had been maimed and left for dead.

And the other thing that got me was that he was only nineteen years old, and I was only sixteen years old, and why had we both suffered so much, well, the devil was having a laugh or two.

I drove and the world was desolate except for some cottonwoods lined against the banks of a river with no name. There were railroad tracks and feed elevators and finally a water tower and some dilapidated tract houses and a sign reading *Welcome to Thompsonville, Home of 1,372 Friendly People.* I exited off of Interstate 6 and came to Main Street and there were boarded-up windows and a bar and a liquor store and a diner and a hardware store.

I parked in front of the hardware store, and it was called Fred's, and there was a dead soldier in my trunk, and I walked inside, and the cashier at the front of the store was a trashy little blonde, and I figured that maybe I could show her a thing or two, but I thought better of it and just nodded politely.

In the front of the store was a round-point shovel, and I grabbed that; then I started wandering up and down the aisles, and I found a mason's jar and a gasoline siphon and a container of Sterno, and I brought this stuff to the cashier and laid down a hundred-dollar bill and she looked at me with a strange expression and she wanted to know what I aimed to do with this stuff and Joseph Downs was dead and Joseph Downs was alive.

CHAPTER 29

Back in the car, still driving west, thinking about Constance and rats and war and insanity and…

The sun was setting and I could feel the darkness before I saw it. Endless miles of frozen dirt and buffalo grass. I could have left him in the wheat fields somewhere to rot away like Mother, but he deserved a proper burial and so did I. Drove a while, found an old abandoned church with crows circling the steeple, and everything was in sepia. I parked a ways away, and I was filled with the power of the Holy Spirit, and I stepped out of the car.

Off in the distance the lightning flashed and a low growl of thunder followed. The headlights shone on the frozen soil, and I pulled out my shovel, and once again I was digging, and in my pockets were flowers for the grave.

Hands bleeding, muscles aching, I pressed on.

Things didn't have to end this way.

My destiny was never chosen for me.

Love was waiting for me.

The hole was dug. Not six feet. Deep enough.

I walked back to the truck, head down, shovel dragging behind me. More lightning and thunder, more wind howling across the plains.

His face was burned and charred, but the pain and sadness were gone forever. I pulled him out of the trunk and as I staggered across the ice-covered ground, grasping the soldier tightly in my arms, I could feel myself transforming, could feel my old soul begin to rise and vanish into the waiting darkness and gloom.

And the other dog tag was still around his neck, and I pulled it off and placed it in my pocket and I pushed him over the edge and he rolled onto his back and he was staring up at me with those terrible eyes and I stared back for a while, and I blinked first; then I picked up the shovel and covered him with dirt and ice and snow and there was no absolution or blessing or prayers.

From partial to complete transformation:

I siphoned gasoline into the mason's jar, half-way full, then opened up the container of Sterno and scooped up a handful and placed it in the jar, used a stick to mix it up. My father said, you never know when they're gonna come for you, you never know, and you can mix napalm with gasoline, and when ignited, it can kill or wound because the napalm will stick, don't you see, and third-degree burns aren't painful because the nerves are killed, but hit someone with a small splash and they'll survive, and they'll be in pain, and they'll have hideous scars, and this should only be used in self-defense, Benton, and Sterno is the same thing as napalm, and you never know when those neo-fascists will come after you, you never know, Benton.

A Comanche warrior, I used my fingers to cover my face with the Sterno/gasoline mixture, and then I sat on the ground and clasped my hands together and prayed for a good long time and I thought about all the hurt and sadness I'd ever felt, and there was no turning back for me this time, Constance, Constance, Constance, Constance.

In my pocket there was a lighter. In the ground was Joseph Downs. On the plains the wind was blowing. Where was the mountain? Far away now. Far away now. Far away now.

And then the flames are everywhere and I'm choking and my eyes are bursting. Muted screams. The squad leader: My fucking leg, my fucking leg! My best friend Dan: Where's help? Where the fuck is help? And then quiet, the world shimmering in reds and oranges and yellows.

Time drifting forward then backward then sideways. And trucks crashing through the flames. Soldiers with gas masks. Joseph Downs in the ground. A soldier appearing in front of me, head jerking spastically, shouting instructions, no sounds heard.

His hand is grasping mine and pulling and I want to stay in the truck in the burning truck where I can rest and be redeemed and he pulls me out, this angel in the night, and a dozen more gas-masked angels hover over me, shaking their heads, and the wind is blowing hard and cold.

I'm lying in the snow, I'm lying in the desert and my face is burning and everything is blurry and the world is dying and I pray to God that I'm dead, and he doesn't listen, and the ground begins to tremble and the Soldier rises, arms stretched, nails in his palm, sanctified at last...

And when he spoke, his voice was only in my head and I covered my ears, but that only made it louder:

Who are you? he said, causing blood to spurt from my nostrils.

Benton Faulk, I said.

No, no, no! Who...are...you?

I don't know.

Don't fuck with me! Who are you? Who the fuck are you?

No answer.

Then he reached into my pocket and pulled out the dog tag and placed it around my neck and my brains were seeping from my ears.

Let's try again. Who are you?

Downs, I mumbled.

I can't hear you. Speak up.

Downs! Joseph Downs!

Better. What happened to your face?

I was wounded in the war. IED.

Yes, yes! Now repeat after me: My name is Joseph Downs.

My name is Joseph Downs.

I served my country proudly.

But I couldn't speak because my mouth was filled with fire.

Say it!

201

I served…

What?

I served…

Keep going!

I served my country…my country…

Yes?

Proudly. I served my country proudly.

And then staggering to the car and hitting the engine and glancing in the rearview mirror. Screams and laughter and screams.

My name is Joseph Downs. I served my country proudly.

PART THREE:
JOSEPH DOWNS (2010)

"There are too many of them; you can't kill the world."
—Davis Grubb, *Night of the Hunter*

CHAPTER 30

I stepped outside of the truck, the snow crunching beneath my bloodstained boots. A bedroom light flashed on, and I saw Lilith in the window. She was wearing a long white gown and her face was otherworldly. I stood in front of my hearse, the shotgun dangling from my hand, a steel appendage. Somewhere in the distance a lonesome train whistle blew. I pulled back my hair with my hand and started walking slowly toward her door. And now I knew what I was going to do, what I had to do. Choices aren't made. There is no free will.

I stood on the porch, listened to the murderous wind chimes in the breeze. I'd been here before. You can't undo the things you've done. The door was unlocked and I opened it slowly. I entered the living room, warped floorboards beneath my feet, a distorted soundtrack. The morning light shone through the curtains, dull and muted. And then I heard Lilith. Victor? she called, fear in her voice. Is that you?

Victor. So that was the *vaquero's* name.

I shook my head, grinned. Not Victor.

I walked through the living room, glancing around, taking in details I hadn't noticed before. An old fireplace, all bricked in. Television on a whiskey carton. Matryoshka dolls on the mantel. A portrait of a dead ancestor on the wall, but no photographs of the living.

Lilith called out again, voice panicked, pleading for her Victor, but he'd gone back to his warm home, left her all alone to face the big bad wolf and other monsters in the light. The shotgun was in my hand. I'd killed men in Iraq. I'd never been to Iraq. Truth? What is truth?

The door to the bedroom was closed and it was too quiet and I knew she was in there. I stood outside the door for a long time, my elongated shadow spreading down the hallway. I pictured her huddled on her bed, eyes full of horror, body trembling, anticipating the coming apocalypse. I knew that terrorized feeling well. How many nights had I lain awake in my own bed and stared at the shadows moving on the wall, listened to rats scurrying on the floor, tasted the blood dripping from my lips, felt that reverberation of dread in my soul? Yes, I knew what she was feeling, and I was more than glad. Any compassion I might have had for the woman had vanished when I'd seen the *vaquero* leaving her house as the sun lifted above the snow-covered plains.

Shotgun at the ready, grin spread across my melted face, I pushed open the door. Lilith was inside, but she wasn't huddled on the bed. She was standing with her back to the door, arms folded, gazing out the window at the bloodshot sky. Her hair was now black, chopped short. She'd gotten a new tattoo on her shoulder blade—Chinese symbols, meaningless. I stood just inside the doorway, lowered my weapon. She knew I was there but didn't turn around. I watched her. How badly I wanted to strangle her, how badly I wanted to fuck her. She was less than human, and aren't we all. When she finally spoke, her voice was soft, sad. I thought you were in jail, she said. They told me you'd be locked up for good.

I leaned against the wall, took a load off. Sympathetic judge, I said. What with me being a war hero and all. An old friend bailed me out. It doesn't matter. Freedom's the worst prison of all.

Lilith nodded her head slowly, traced her finger down the window. And what are you going to do, Joseph? Rape me? Kill me?

Maybe.

She turned around, raven hair untamed, face smeared with last night's makeup. Her eyes narrowed as she stared at my face, then my gun, and then back at my face. Her lips spread into a grin and she laughed. God, she said, you really are gruesome.

And what can a fellow say to that? She was cold and hard and mean. I took a few steps so that I was standing right in front of her. Our eyes locked and neither of us blinked. Then she loaded up and spat a good one directly into my face. I wiped the spit off with the back of my hand, thought about it for a second. Blood burning behind my eyes, I gripped the barrel of the shotgun and swung hard, connecting flush with her cheekbone. She staggered backward, spun around, and then collapsed to the floor, a rag doll that nobody wanted anymore. I took another step forward until I was looming over her. She was in bad shape, moaning and groaning, grabbing at her face, writhing in pain. I almost felt bad about what I'd done, but then I remembered the world and the way it was, and I reared back and kicked her hard in the stomach. She grunted and gasped and I kicked her one more time, then let her be. That was all the loathing I could muster.

I walked over to the bed, sat down on covers and sheets all twisted together from last night's sin-fest, and pulled out a can of snuff. I snorted a healthy pinch, sneezed a couple of times. I watched her all curled up in the fetus position, sobbing silently. Five, maybe ten minutes passed before she finally pulled herself to a sitting position. She moved against the wall, beneath the window. Her face was a pulpy mess. Got a cigarette? she asked.

I reached into my shirt pocket and tossed her my last bent cigarette and a lighter. She lit it and inhaled deeply, eyes drifting back into her skull. She smoked greedily, quickly. She didn't look scared anymore, just resigned. Did that make you feel good? she said.

I shrugged my shoulders. There's no pleasure in inflicting pain, I said.

She blew out some smoke from the corner of her mouth, said, So what's next?

Don't know, I said. Maybe you can start by telling me the truth and we can go from there.

Truth? What version of the truth are you looking for?

The only one. Tell me about Victor the *Vaquero*. More than just a fling on a lonely night, huh?

She looked up at me, bemused. Yeah, she said. More than just a fling.

How long?

Three years. On and off.

I got up from the bed, paced across the room. Lilith sucked on her cigarette and watched me from the corner of her eye.

And your husband. Nick? He wasn't as abusive as you made him out to be, was he?

Smoke trickled from her nostrils and she half grinned. I don't know what you're talking about. You saw the way he was in the bar, the day we met.

Yeah. I saw. But that night, when you showed up at my hotel room, all bloody and swollen. He didn't do that, did he?

Lilith crushed out her cigarette on the floor and shook her head. No, she said. He didn't do that.

Then...

Victor gave me the beating. But it was my idea. Every last punch.

Your idea, huh?

You were too hesitant to do what you needed to do. I needed you to be mad. Mad enough to kill.

So it was all a setup.

Not a setup. An opportunity. Surely you can't blame a young woman for taking an opportunity.

I laughed at that. An opportunity? You killed your husband. And for what? A little insurance money?

Correction. You killed my husband. And don't be so cynical. It's not just about the money. I might love Victor. He might be a good man.

I shook my head, said, There's no such thing as a good man. We're all guilty from the time we're born, and what God ought to do is stop us before we ever get going.

That's a pretty sentiment, Joseph.

It's not a pretty world, now, is it?

I didn't say anything else for a while and neither did she. I felt tired, very tired. Finally said, There's something else I want to know. Something I've been wondering about.

Yeah?

Why me? Why'd you choose me?

Lilith stared at me for a long moment, and then she shook her head. Boy, you are stupid, aren't you?

I never did anything to you. I was only trying to help you.

Help me? Wow, you're so noble, Joseph. Trying to protect me from my husband. Trying to protect the country from the terrorists. What a hero! Only I didn't need your protection. I needed your violence. See how useful you can be?

She was goading me on, that much I knew, but somehow I couldn't muster any more rage. Because she was right. She'd played me for a fool and won. And so had my country.

I could have cut my losses right then and there. Accepted my fate and walked out the door. Let Lilith live, let Victor live, wait for the jaws of justice to clamp around my throat. But I couldn't. Because the truth is that a man's gotta believe in something, whether it's God or love or justice. And I believed in retribution.

This Victor, I said. Where does he live?

What do you want to know that for?

Cause we're gonna pay him a little visit, that's why.

A little visit, huh? And then what? Gonna beat him up? Gonna show me what a man you are?

Don't know yet. Might. Might not. Nothing much to lose, one way or another.

She nodded her head slowly, wiped the wisps of hair from her eyes. No, she said. Nothing much to lose.

CHAPTER 31

My mind was splintering and my memories were somebody else's. War scenes from a B-movie.

Lilith drove the pickup. She'd changed into blue jeans and a flannel shirt. The shotgun was on my lap and bubblegum pop was on the radio.

The sun shone, reflecting a kaleidoscope of light off the snow. We didn't talk because there was nothing to say. And it was better that way. People are better off just keeping their mouths shut.

We drove through town, down Baker Street, a few blocks east of Main. Victor lived in a little tract house decorated by poverty. Collapsed metal fence. Laundry hanging from a frozen wire. Broken-down El Camino on blocks. Skeletal cottonwood. We parked across the street, behind a crippled Mexican working under the hood of his car, crutches beneath his arms, filthy children at his feet.

Lilith turned off the engine, kept her hand on the wheel. She stared straight ahead, face showing a little strain, shoulders rising and falling with each breath. She said: Well, here we are, hero. Have you made up your mind yet? Decided what you're gonna do? Decided how you're gonna show me your manhood?

I looked at her, shook my head. Just gonna have a little talk is all.

A little talk?

That's right. I'm not gonna hurt him. Just want to set some things straight.

She had no choice but to believe me. We got out of the car, her clutching her stomach, me the shotgun. The cripple looked up from the hood of his car and froze. I nodded at him, a friendly nod, and he nodded back.

An American flag hung from the front of the house, whipping in the wind. We walked up the rotted front porch. I glanced in the window. The television was turned on, but nobody was there to watch it.

I turned to Lilith. Got a key?

Yes.

Give it to me.

She fumbled around in her purse for a while before locating the key. She handed it to me. After jiggling it around for a while, the lock clicked and I pushed open the door. The sound of the show's laugh track echoed eerily throughout the lonely room.

Aside from the television stand and an old gray couch, there was no furniture. The white walls were blank and peeling in some places. A pair of tan work boots sat askew next to the door. Just in front of the television stand, there was a narrow sloping hall that led to the small kitchen.

Lilith and I walked down the hallway, me pressing the shotgun against her back. I peered into the kitchen. A teakettle and an empty metal pot rested on an ancient-looking stove. On the far side of the kitchen, a pair of large windows looked out onto the neighbors' backyard, where an old pit bull was chained to the fence. A single lightbulb dangled from the ceiling. In the middle of the room stood a round, wooden table, covered by a red-and-white-checkered tablecloth. On the kitchen table sat three bottles of Budweiser. Two were empty and the third had just a swallow left. A cigarette burned in an ashtray, the smoke swaying to the ceiling in a crazy gypsy dance. Four mismatched chairs surrounded the table. And sitting on one of the chairs was Victor. He was sharpening an electrician's knife, his right hand moving back and forth like a violinist. When he looked up, saw the shotgun, his dirt-brown eyes became wild-looking.

Morning, Victor, I said. Lilith looked at him and shook her head, suddenly the helpless victim.

He rose to his feet, waving the knife in his hand.

I raised the shotgun, aimed it at his oversized belt bucket. Put it down, Victor, I said.

For a few moments, he made no move, then his fingers loosened and the knife clattered to the ground. Go pick it up, I said to Lilith. She walked across the kitchen floor, bent down and picked it up. I reached out my hand. She glanced apologetically at Victor, then handed me the weapon. I stuck it in the back of my pants.

I stood there for a while, biding my time, trying to make up my mind. You didn't treat me very fairly, I said.

He shook his head. I'm sorry. It was nothing personal.

You coulda killed him yourself. Then everybody would have been happy. Everybody but Nick, that is.

He didn't say anything, just stared at me, wondering just how murderous a fellow I was.

Got any rope, Victor?

He thought for a moment, eyes rolling into the back of his head. No, he said. No rope. Got bungee cords, though.

Go get 'em.

So we left the kitchen and walked down the hallway, toward his bedroom, Victor the *Vaquero* in the lead, Lilith the Whore next, Joseph the Soldier last.

I stood in the doorway and watched as he reached under his bed and pulled out a half dozen or so bungee cords of various colors and lengths. He tossed them on the bed, then looked up at me, eyes full of dread.

I pointed toward a wooden chair in the corner of the room, told him to sit. He did as he was told. And that's when Lilith broke down, dirty mascara tears sliding down her cheeks. It might have been an act, probably was an act. I didn't care anymore. What are you gonna do? she sobbed. You said you weren't gonna hurt him.

I'm not gonna hurt him, I said again, and I meant what I said.

Then what are you doing this for, huh?

I didn't answer. While Lilith stood there crying

tears of deceit, I used the bungee cords to tie Victor to the chair. He didn't struggle much, didn't try to wiggle his way out. I didn't gag him; there was no need. Then I stood next to him, raised the shotgun vaguely. Lilith covered her mouth with her hand. I squeezed the Mexican's shoulder, said, You love her?

He nodded his head.

Why? She's a wicked woman. The worst sinner I've ever known, and I've known my share of sinners.

He shrugged his shoulders, didn't answer.

Come here, I said to Lilith.

Following my command, she shuffled slowly toward where I was standing, her eyes done crying, now only filled with loathing. All the smugness had vanished from her demeanor.

Kiss him, I said.

What, you wanna jerk off?

Kiss him, I said again.

She made no move so I raised the shotgun. Fucking pervert, she said, then moved next to him, bent down and kissed him on the lips. Both of them kept their eyes open, no passion.

I said: Now he dies.

Victor took it in stride, only raising his eyebrow, frowning slightly. Lilith, meanwhile, became belligerent.

Fuck you! she cried. You're a lying bastard. You promised you wouldn't hurt him. Goddamn lying bastard!

I grinned, said, Don't worry, sunshine. I'm not going to break my promise. I'm not going to kill him. You are. You're going to slit his fucking throat.

At first, Lilith didn't believe me. She shook her

head and laughed, like I was doing stand-up at Caroline's. Even when I pulled out the electrician's knife and placed it in her pretty little hand, she kept right on laughing.

It wasn't until I slapped her hard across the face that the laughter ceased and the sobbing returned. She dropped the knife to the floor and fell to her knees.

Pick up the knife, I said.

Fuck you.

Do as he says, the *vaquero* said.

Wiping away more brown tears, body shaking, she bent down and grabbed the knife.

You're crazy if you think I'm going to hurt him, she said.

I cocked the shotgun and aimed it at her forehead. You'll kill him, I said. Or else I'll kill the both of you.

Victor piped up again. Don't do this. They'll find you. And they'll hang you. We'll give you the money if that's what you want. All of it. $250,000.

I don't want your money, I whispered. Only your blood.

Lilith changed strategies. Went for the heartstrings. Joseph. Please. Think about what you're doing. Think about me. When you came to that bar and saw Nick knocking me around, you stood up for me. You protected me. You don't have to murder anymore. You can save three lives today.

I turned toward the whore, said, He who knows how to save lives best knows how to destroy them. Which brings me to this point. The movies have taught you all wrong. When you stand behind someone to slit his throat, don't pull his head backward.

Corrosion

What you need to do is push his head forward, bring those vessels together. That way, he'll be dead in minutes, not hours.

She shook her head. Where did you learn all of that, Joseph?

The Marines, that's where! 1st Battalion, 7th Regiment, 1st Division! Stationed in Mosul! I served, damn it! I served with honor!

Then I raised the shotgun again and clenched my teeth. It's time, I said. It's time for this goddamn wetback to bleed. Make up your mind. And think wisely, Lilith. You don't do it, I'll blow your goddamn brains out, so help me God.

Fuck you, she said again, but the spunk was gone. I'm not gonna kill him.

Victor nodded his head. It's okay, Lilith, he said. Do it. Kill me. Save your own life. Jesus awaits me!

Everything happened quickly then. My mind couldn't keep up. Little snippets. Lilith lunging forward. The knife slashing across his throat. Blood spilling over his chest. Body twitching, eyes wide in agony. Lilith collapsing to the floor, the bloody knife clattering next to her. And then silence, God hanging from a noose.

CHAPTER 32

I pulled Lilith to her feet, held her close to me, felt her breath and the blood in her veins. She wasn't crying, just staring straight ahead. Dead, was all she said. And I couldn't argue with her.

There were no fingerprints to wipe down, no DNA to remove. They'd figure out who did it, but they'd never find us. Not where we were going.

I held the shotgun with one hand and Lilith with the other. We staggered across the street toward the truck. The cripple who'd been working on his car was gone and the streets were deserted.

I tossed the shotgun in the bed and helped Lilith into the truck. Any fight she'd had was gone — her body was limp, her eyes empty. I hit the engine and thought things over. Nick McClellan was dead and so was Victor *Vaquero*, and I was alive and Lilith wouldn't leave me.

And then we were back on the chimney smoke highway, and it was cold and gray and lonely, which is the way things are on the plains in November. Dead leaves and crows and radio static and hair slicked back with Wild Root Cream Oil.

Lilith rested her head on the glass, face pale and sickly. Her flannel shirt was covered with Victor's blood. There were spatters on her face and hands, too. Sins that could never be washed away. We drove in silence.

Well, we must have gone 20 miles or so when we came upon this ramshackle trading post. The wooden structure was rotting, and weeds grew through the broken pavement. A hand-painted sign read *Cowboy Bob's*. I parked the truck behind an old rusted Mercury Coup, told Lilith that I'd be keeping an eye on her, but she was too far gone to respond. I went inside and bought a package of beef jerky, a can of Rooster dip, a package of hand wipes, and a sweatshirt with a picture of a wolf on it. I asked the one-armed dwarf of a cashier if I could use the phone and he said there was a pay phone on the side of the building. I thanked him, walked outside, located the phone. I dialed a number that I'd never forgotten. 719-522-1638. I let it ring 10, 12 times. No answer. I slammed down the receiver and strode back to the car.

Lilith stared straight ahead, eyes still as dead as could be. I pulled out some wipes, tried cleaning the blood off her hands and face. No good. Then I handed her the sweatshirt and told her to change. She didn't hear me. She just kept staring.

The hearse engine was noisy, but the pickup drove smoothly. The fellow at the auto shop had done good work and I was glad I hadn't given up on the old truck. I drove a good ten miles below the speed limit because I didn't want to get pulled over. Outside, the world was stark and gray, the landscape a shoddy charcoal painting. Skeleton trees stretched out with contorted branches, and sagging telephone wires swayed in the wind. And there an abandoned and burned farmhouse surrounded by dying alfalfa and junkyard automobiles. Ravens and vultures skulked up ahead, waiting, waiting. Off in the distance, the silhouette of the mountains was getting closer and closer.

As we drove, I kept glancing in my rearview mirror, waiting for the flashing lights, but Sheriff Baker was nowhere to be seen. I found a country music station on the radio. It was filled with static and kept fading in and out. Sometimes a man speaking in hallucinogenic Spanish would cut in, then it would shift back to music. Snow fell slantways. Lilith's eyes closed, and she slept fitfully.

Another hour and we were in the foothills, driving through winding roads surrounded by lodgepoles and pine trees and aspens, an occasional lonely log cabin on a rutted path. The windshield wipers slapped away the snow and soon the voices on the radio were gone and it was just static. We drove higher and higher, the snowcapped mountains towering ominously. I drank some brandy and chewed some tobacco, trying to relax myself. There were no other cars, and I kept worrying that I was dead. How long had it been? Why was I coming back?

The sky was the color of champagne and my eyes were kaleidoscope lenses. There was a strange magnetic force, pulling me toward my destiny, toward that evil place. I couldn't have turned around if I had wanted to. A couple of times Lilith jerked awake, remembered the narrative, and closed her eyes, a single tear escaping from beneath her lashes.

I drove slowly, concentrating on the winding road. I tried hard not to think about death and destruction, but it was no use. Nightmares were my waking state now.

And after some time, we came upon the vestiges of a living ghost town, the junkyard of cars at the entrance providing a symbolic barricade from unwanted visitors. And then a wooden sign, faded and weather-beaten. *Silverville. Elevation 9,228 Feet.* Hands gripping the steering wheel, knuckles white, I drove slowly past the broken-down jalopies, and onto Gold Street. Nothing quaint here, just a handful of worn-out brick buildings, including a little restaurant called the Miner's Café.

My breathing quickened and sweat dribbled from my forehead, stinging my eyes. *They'll never find us.* I parked the car out front of the restaurant, shook Lilith awake. Time to eat, I said.

Her eyes fluttered open and she watched me with that dead expression. I'm not hungry, she said.

You've gotta eat, I said. Don't know when our next meal will be.

I opened the door and stepped outside, then opened the passenger-side door and helped Lilith out. The air was cold and my breath was thick.

We walked slowly toward the restaurant and ghosts were whispering in my ear. I pushed open the door and we stepped inside. It was a peculiar-looking place, a hoarder's dream. There were cow and elk and bison heads stuck to the wall, and there was a telephone booth and a saddle and a wooden cowboy and a wooden stove. There was a rifle and a mining lantern and a saloon door and paintings of people long dead. And hanging from the ceiling: a chandelier, a noose, and a snarling wolf.

Our feet echoed on the hardwood floor. The usual cast of characters was sitting at the counter: a skinny man with frightened eyes and an Elmer Fudd hat; a fat man with mutton chops and a NASCAR leather jacket; another fat man with a beard and a lumberjack shirt; and Miss Lonelyheart, face full of heartache. And standing alone in the corner with a candy cigarette dangling from his mouth, a stooped old man with a dustbowl face and aviator shades.

We sat down at a long picnic table in the middle of the café. Nobody paid us any mind, not even the waitress, a woman with balding hair and missing teeth. I handed Lilith a menu, but she dropped it on the table. Time passed. The waitress ignored us.

Eventually I rose to my feet and made my way to the counter. The waitress finished joking with the customers and nodded at me. What can I get for you, darlin'? She studied the torment in my eyes and the scar tissue on my face and I could see that she was more than a little bit frightened of the monster in her presence.

Two coffees and two slices of cherry pie, I said.

Be coming right up, she said.

And then from the corner: I seen ya before! Right here in Silverville! With my own eyes! It was the stooped old man, ranting, his back toward me, hands fluttering in the air like moths.

Shaking my head, I returned to the table and sat down. Lilith stared straight ahead, face expressionless and soul missing, like one of those lobotomy patients from long ago. Outside, the wind moaned like a Halloween ghost. A few minutes later, the waitress came and slid a couple of healthy slices of pie on the table. Then she poured the mud, offered us some cream. And just to make conversation: You two from around here or just passing through?

Lilith opened her mouth like she was going to say something, but nothing came out. She closed her mouth and blinked slowly. Haven't decided, I said.

Hey, Betty, I'm running a little dry, one of the fat men shouted.

The waitress returned to her clientele, and I drank my coffee and ate my pie. Lilith didn't even glance at her food. Instead her eyes were fixated on something behind me. I turned around. On the back wall, behind the register, was an oversized portrait of a red-headed woman, surrounded by flowers and saints and crosses. I felt my chest tighten.

That woman…she said, her voice dreamy.

I tried distracting her, pushed the piece of pie her way.

That woman…Lilith said again, this time loud enough for the waitress to hear her.

The balding waitress looked up at the portrait, then sighed and shook her head. Name's Constance Durban, she said. She used to work here.

Used to work here? What happened to her?

She disappeared.

Disappeared?

I couldn't figure Lilith's interest. Her eyes shone brightly, her soul momentarily back in place.

The waitress flashed a conspiratorial smile. Don't let the hushed setting fool you. Silverville is a hamlet of sins, a million secrets buried alive.

Did somebody hurt her? Lilith asked.

The other folks at the counter all gave us sideways glances. Miss, said the skinny man with the Elmer Fudd hat, it's best not to talk about those things. Best not to reopen wounds.

Then maybe you should take down the picture, I said.

Sure as hell know him! shouted the crazy man in the corner. Known him since he was a lad! The devil he is, plain and simple!

You hush, Kyle! the waitress said in a firm voice, and he shut up but quick.

After that, nobody talked for a while and the mood was solemn. I finished my coffee and pie, got to work on Lilith's. That woman...she said again.

I threw down my fork, wiped my mouth. When I spoke again, my own words surprised me. It was like another person speaking. You know an old man named Flan Faulk?

Nobody answered, heads bent down.

I heard he went crazy. Stories of rats and rotting corpses. Did he go crazy?

Silence. I nodded at Lilith. Let's get out of here, I said. You go on outside, wait in the truck. I'm gonna pay. Lilith did as she was told. I kept an eye on her as she walked to the truck, opened the door, and sat inside. No longer conniving, just obedient.

I walked up to the counter, threw down a twenty

on the table. Yes, sir, I said. I heard he went crazy and I heard his son went crazy, too. Butchered Constance Durban. Buried her body in the side of the mountain. Do I have the story right?

The waitress looked up from wiping the counter. She was thrown off guard. You've got some nerve, mister.

I only ask because I knew the both of them, a long time ago.

Miss Lonelyheart looked up from her iced tea, snarled. Yeah, you got the story about right. They were lunatics, the both of them.

And they never found young Benton, did they?

Everybody looked at each other, but nobody answered.

And they never found Constance Durban, neither?

More silence.

And Flan Faulk?

Mr. NASCAR spit a stream of brown tobacco into a cup. Then he said, Them Denver doctors let him out. Figgered he wasn't crazy no more. You ask me, they figgered wrong. He's back in Silverville. At his old place. Keeps to hisself, mostly.

I nodded my head, said, I'm much obliged, and started walking toward the door. I could feel a roomful of eyes staring at the back of my head.

I'd just turned the doorknob when I felt somebody grab my shoulder. I spun around, came face-to-face with the crazy old man. I knew who you was from the moment you set foot in here! I never forget a face! You're the boy who did the killin'! Then he pulled off his sunglasses and his eyes darted spastically back and forth across his sockets. The eyes of a blind man.

CHAPTER 33

Outside the temperature had dropped 20 degrees at least. I opened the truck door and stepped inside. Lilith sat in the passenger seat, rocking back and forth like an Orthodox Jew praying at the Wailing Wall. Then she turned to me and said, I know that girl. The one in the photograph.

I shook my head. No, you don't.

Yes, she said. She's me. Who I'll become.

I hit the engine and drove. George Jones sang on the radio. "He Stopped Loving Her Today." The station was full of static, but he sounded better that way. Up the mountain we went, snow falling harder.

Where are we going? Lilith said. Where are you taking me?

I turned and looked at her and for the first time I saw the truth, God's revelation, and I knew that Lilith was the devil, that Constance was the devil, that my mother was the devil.

We're going home, I said.

*   *   *

Twenty minutes passed, maybe more, before we came to an old valley surrounded by a crown of trees. Then the old mining cabin appeared through the canopy like a drunken dream, all indistinct and hazy. Four walls built out of logs, a wooden shake roof, a door, and a pair of boarded-up windows. And just beyond the cabin, an abandoned mine, the rotted boards collapsed on the shaft like a jigsaw of bones.

I felt an ancient coldness rise up inside of me. I let off the gas, and the truck rolled to a stop. We sat in the pickup for a long time, me just staring at the cabin, Lilith staring at me. Then the windshield was covered with snow and I couldn't see anymore.

There were ghosts in that cabin. Men who came to the mountains with nothing but a pick, a shovel, some food, and a jug of whiskey. Digging and drinking and dying. Murder and suicide. Remember Miles Stockton? Taking a break from beating on his pregnant wife to shoot himself in the temple, leaving the poor woman to clean his brain and blood from the wall. Those ghosts never leave, not really.

I turned off the engine, opened the door. Where are you going? Lilith asked.

I'm going to go check it out, I said. Make sure there aren't any animals inside.

Please, Lilith said.

Please what?

Please...take me home.

Baby, you are home.

I walked slowly toward the mining cabin and the fury was buried in my soul.

The front door was all boarded up. *Walk away. There's no redemption here.* Breathing heavily, I raised my leg and slammed my boot against the wood. It was rotted and splintered easily. After five or so more kicks, the wood was pretty well broken through. I pushed the smashed door out of the way and stepped inside.

The act of breaking open the door filled the shack with dust rising in the slatted sunlight. Shoulders heaving, I studied my surroundings. A cracked lightbulb hung perilously from the ceiling. There was a wood-burning stove and a gas lantern and a wooden chair and a small cot. I walked farther inside, the boards creaking under my feet. Then I stopped, stood there for a while, dread oozing everywhere. In the back of the cabin, wood piled high. I knew there was no turning back. Redemption is a song for the delusional. Sweat dribbling down my forehead, I got busy pulling off the firewood. Beneath it all was an old miner's rug, tattered and torn. I tossed it aside, saw the small padlocked door on the ground, layered with dust and grime. I stood staring at that hatch for some time, just thinking and thinking. Hands trembling, I removed the chain from around my neck, unsnapped a key away from the dog tag. *Get out, soldier. The walls are collapsing.* I dropped to my knees, gripped the key tightly. *Get out.* I pushed the key into the lock and turned. It clicked open. After tossing the lock aside, I grabbed a hold of the edge of the hatch and lifted it up, letting it slam behind me on the wooden floor. I gazed downward. A long, darkened ladder. Something terrible in me. *Get out, soldier! That's an order.*

I walked across the room and grabbed the gas lantern. Kerosene still inside. I opened the shield and lit the flame with my lighter. My hands still trembled and the ocean still boiled. Wheezing steadily, maggots crawling beneath my skin, I turned and walked out of the cabin, back toward the truck where Lilith's face had vanished beneath the snow-covered windshield.

I opened the passenger's-side door. Lilith's eyes shone with rage and they could see every sin I'd ever committed.

It's time to go, I said.

You don't have to do this.

We've come this far. No sense in turning back now.

She had a hard time walking. Nerves maybe. She kept falling into the snow. I'd kind of drag her for a while, then pull her back to her feet. I saw that she was crying. I slapped the tears out of her. That tooth in my mouth was aching, rotting. The rats were gnawing on my brain.

Inside the Skull Shack. Lilith inconsolable. What is this? she said, fear, fear, fear. Who lives here?

I grinned, said, You live here. But she didn't get it.

Please, she said. Joseph...

Devils, I said. Then I pointed toward the open hatch. We're gonna go down there, I said. Have a look-see.

Lilith shook her head. No, she said. Not this way.

I'm sorry, but there's no other way. I didn't want it to end like this. Honest I didn't. I grabbed her by the arm, pulled her toward the ladder. But you gotta sleep in the bed you made.

She looked up at me with the same stare I'd seen so many times before. We'd all seen ghosts, every last one of us. I shone the kerosene lamp toward the ladder. Lilith peered downward. Wha…what's down there? she said, dirty tears rolling down her face.

I don't know.

Slowly, we made our way down the wooden ladder. It smelled damp and dank. My legs felt rubbery and I thought I might collapse. Lilith held on to my arm, digging her fingers into my ligaments. She wouldn't stop crying.

We finally reached the bottom. I raised the lantern, shone it around. I looked at the ground, saw an old mattress covered in shit and blood and maggots. Lilith began to faint. I held her up.

I took another step forward. And that's when I heard moaning, soft and low, and came face-to-face with the monster.

A nightmarish vision, its hair and teeth missing, eyes sockets empty, a bloated purple tongue lolling between swollen and bloody lips. Skin sloughed from a shriveled little body, spine badly contorted, arms and legs gnarled.

Help me, the monster cried in a little girl's voice, as Lilith fell to the floor. The monster stood over her. Please. Help me.

I lost control, screaming, crying, screaming. My soul was disintegrating by the second. But Lilith didn't see anything, saying, What is it, Joseph, what is it?

In my panic, I dropped the lantern and it crashed on the ground, glass splintering everywhere. I was a blind man, falling apart, making my way up the ladder. I didn't look back, but I could hear moaning and screeches of terror. I pulled myself out of the dugout and rolled to my back. I struggled to my feet and started lifting the hatch. Lilith and the monster were right behind me. I had to kick at them with my boot to keep them down. Finally, I got the hatch shut and locked. They were pounding on the hatch, the both of them. Body trembling, I backed away slowly, then turned around and staggered out of the shack.

Soon the pounding and the screams became more and more muffled and then the world was quiet, gone, gone forever.

CHAPTER 34

Memories get mixed up memories change one
person remembers it one way somebody else remembers it a different way I grew up in a small Ohio town
my parents died in a car crash *remember the rats and
the sickness mother was withering away* I was almost at
the mountain when the engine gave out *the Christ rat
especially* as soon as those buildings collapsed I knew
I wanted to be a soldier *everyone said he was crazy I said
they were crazy* I was in Mosul we were driving down
the road and it was midnight it was pitch-black and
our lights were off we were wearing night-vision
goggles *how far you going partner he said and his face
was melted* as soon as I saw those buildings collapse
I knew I wanted to be a soldier *as far as you can take
me* she reminded me of somebody that was certain
Constance Constance Constance we were driving down
this road and there was this tiny bridge over a little

canal and one moment you're whole and beautiful *from the darkness in the sea to the sunshine on the hill in the forest filled with trees my shadow has gone still* I grew up on the mountain I grew up in a small Ohio town *nobody would miss him I thought it's perfect* I grew up in a small Ohio town *what do you need the Sterno for the woman said its just like napalm it'll burn your skin good if you're not careful* my name is Joseph Downs here's my dog collar with my name on it I served my country proudly *as far as you'll take me I said* Nick Mc-Clellan deserved to die Lilith deserved to die *Mother deserved to die* memories get mixed up I was badly injured unrecognizable *his face was melted* my name is Joseph Downs *my name is Benton Faulk* I served my country proudly.

CHAPTER 35

I sat in the truck outside of the Skull Shack. The hearse engine was humming but I didn't drive, couldn't drive. Instead, I just sat there studying my face in the rearview mirror, trying to find something, the truth maybe, but the truth was vile. The past changes and we forget. I reached behind my head, ripped off my dog tag, and placed it in the palm of my hand. I stared at the name for a good long time. Joseph Downs. Then my fingers tightened around the identification tag, and my eyes clenched shut. I squeezed harder and harder until the tag sliced right through the palm of my hand, drew blood. I watched in bewilderment as the blood dripped like a faucet onto the upholstery.

Eventually I pushed the truck into gear and hit the gas. I drove around for a long time, Lilith's screams echoing in my ears. I felt weary. I needed to lay my head somewhere.

Down the mountain a ways, I came upon a little motel, hidden beneath the pine trees. The vacancy light shone and I parked in front of the office next to an old Plymouth with suicide doors. I walked slowly to the motel and my hand was covered with blood.

The office door was closed and locked. I pounded on the door a few times and waited. Some time passed before an old lady with long gray hair and a long gray nightgown appeared. Her face was groggy as she peered out the window. She unlocked the door and opened it. It's late, she said.

Can you give me a room? I said. I've been traveling all day.

She sighed. All right. Come on in.

In the corner of the office there was a potbelly stove burning and I walked over and warmed my hands. It's getting cold, I said.

She saw the blood on my hand, and her eyes narrowed. You okay there, son?

Sure, I said. Never better.

She handed me a key. Room three, she said. Check out is eleven. That'll be thirty-eight dollars.

I pulled out my wallet and handed her the money. Sorry for waking you, I said. I just need a few hours of sleep.

Don't worry about it, sugar. You have a good night.

The room was basic. A bed, a dresser, a toilet, a sink. No artwork. No television. I got out of my clothes and lay on the bed.

I slept; I don't know for how long. I didn't dream.

When I woke up, the sheets were drenched with sweat. Outside the sun was shining and the sky was a brilliant blue. The snow was starting to melt. It seemed like a long time since I'd seen Lilith. It had only been ten hours. I hoped she was okay. It's a hell of a thing being trapped that way.

I ate breakfast with the old woman and her husband back in their kitchen. Scrambled eggs, bacon, and toast. They were very generous. The husband looked younger than his wife but he had a big goiter lump on his neck. Neither of them asked about my face. They asked other questions though. Where I was from. What I was doing in the mountains. Made me uncomfortable. I became verbally abusive. She got on the phone, called the sheriff's office, or maybe just pretended to call. I stormed out, cursing.

After I left, I felt bad. They were nice people. I never meant to hurt anybody.

*   *   *

The truth about my father. He wasn't crazy. Even though my mother was untrue, even though she betrayed their love, he loved her with all of his body and soul until the end of the world. She got sick and nobody would help her. Not even God, who just sat in his gold leaf recliner, giggling, pointing a bony finger at the Faulk family, saying, The cruelty of man is only equaled by the cruelty of God.

So what could my father do? He'd been on the Mountain his whole life. A carpenter by trade. What did he know of disease and medicines and cures? He was no doctor, but he taught himself medicine. He was no scientist, but he taught himself science. Nobody else cared. They would have let her wither

away, a raisin in the sun. Not my father. He wasn't
crazy. He was in love.

*   *   *

I sat on the tire-swing hanging from the frost-covered pine tree, sucked on tobacco, and stared at the
old house, the yellow paint peeling, the single pitch
roof ready to collapse, a house marked by sorry dilapidation and decay. The lights shone dully behind
the curtains.

Eventually, I made my way along a broken path
until I came to the front door. My shadow stretched
out long and menacing. I pulled out the chewing tobacco from my mouth and flung it on the ground.
Then I rapped on the door a few times and waited.
No footsteps, but a faint voice. The door is open...

I pushed open the door and stepped inside. Except for the ticking of a longcase clock, everything
was quiet. Slowly, zombie-like, I walked across the
living room. I glanced up; saw old photographs on
the mantel. I pulled one off and studied it, that familiar nausea and repulsion spreading through my
body. A young family. Husband, wife, son. The man
wearing a flannel shirt and jeans, a thick mustache
on his face, lips upturned in domestic contentment.
The woman in a long flower dress, black hair pulled
back into a sloppy ponytail, a mischievous twinkle
in her eyes. And the boy, eight maybe nine years old,
cowlick in his hair, grinning goofily, unaware of the
future, unaware of the death and despair that would
surround him for the rest of his days, unaware of the
sickness that would destroy his mother, the corrosion

of her body, the corrosion of his father's mind, the corrosion of his own soul.

I used to not believe in God, his father had said, but now, I'm a changed man, a true believer. Only a Supreme Being could create such misery and mayhem.

And now this man known as Joseph Downs, a man who'd fought and fallen in the desert, stood outside the bedroom, the very bedroom his father had kept locked all those months while his mother had suffered and died and putrefied. Open the door, soldier. Then peel off your soul with a paring knife.

Flan Faulk sat on edge of the bed. His strawlike hair was disheveled, peppered with bald spots from his own yanking. His face was the color of yellowed newspaper except the broken blood vessels around his eyes. He wore no clothes, save for striped tube socks, and his hairy gut hung over his shriveled cock. He stared intently at some imagined point on the floor.

Downs stood in the doorway, a monstrous figure. Everything was quiet and still. Faulk didn't look up, and one might have thought him dead but for his massive stomach rising up and down. Downs took a few more steps into the bedroom, paused, and then continued until he was standing directly over the old man. Now, at last, Faulk looked up, briefly met Downs' gaze.

Do you know who I am? Downs asked.

No answer.

Downs sat down on the bed, placed the man's cold hand in his. Do you know who I am? he said again.

Once again, Faulk looked up, stared into the horrific face. Then, slowly, barely perceptibly, he nodded his head, once, twice.

After that, neither of them spoke for some time. A narrow gauge train whistle blew, and it was a ghost train racing down a track of bones. Then the train was gone, lost in the forest, and the grandfather clock played "Westminster Quarters."

Downs held the old man's hand, squeezed it tightly. Faulk stared at the hands intertwined, eyes glassy. His mouth opened slightly and he seemed to be on the verge of saying something, but there were no words.

Downs glanced up, and then, for just a moment, he saw a strange man standing behind the window, a man with a white physician's jacket, thick spectacles, neatly trimmed mustache. In one hand he held a pipe, in the other an ice pick...

When the old man spoke, his voice startled Joseph Downs, for it was clear and deep and mournful. He said: Your mother. She's very sick. You won't be able to see her. Not today. Not for a long time. Then Faulk squeezed his lips shut, and Joseph Downs noticed a single teardrop roll down his jaundiced cheek.

Downs rose to his feet, looked out the window. *Don't you wonder what became of her? Don't you sometimes hear the crows circling and wonder if she might still be down there?*

And now Faulk stared up at the wounded soldier with eyes full of nothing, and Downs' shadow spread across him, a hooded cloak. The old man shielded his eyes, as if blinded by the gruesome face. Joseph Downs smiled and there was no pleasure in the smile.

Corrosion

He bent down and picked up a pillow, held it in both hands, and Faulk must have sensed what was going to happen. He lay down on the bed, hands folded across his chest, eyes suddenly alert. Maybe, Downs said, there's a heaven for people like us. I reckon not. He brought the pillow down and pressed it against Faulk's face, and at first the old man didn't react, but after a time he started struggling and fighting, kicking his legs and punching his arms. How much time passed? Several minutes perhaps, but eventually the body was still, and Joseph Downs pulled back the pillow and placed it back on the bed.

Flan Faulk's eyes were open wide and so was his mouth, an eternal scream. Downs slumped down onto the bed, next to the lifeless body. He sat there for a long time, hands trembling. Then he closed the old man's eyes with his thumbs. Icy sunlight shone into the room. And Joseph Downs, the war hero, laid his head on the corpse's chest and listened to the wind and the clock and the crows.

PART FOUR:
REVEREND WELLS
(2011)

"And the Earth died screaming."
— Tom Waits

CHAPTER 36

For ten long years I'd driven back and forth across the country in my old pickup truck, listening to The Blackwood Family and The Lefevre Trio, stopping only when the Good Lord told me to stop. Then I'd get out of my truck, stretch my long body, and wander through the streets and bars and whorehouses, gathering up sinners, and the words of the Lord would flow from my mouth with the speed and articulation of an auctioneer, words soaked in kerosene and blood. And sometimes passersby would ignore me, and sometimes they'd stop and snicker, and sometimes they'd stare mesmerized. And perhaps some mistook me for an actor or a street performer, but make no mistake: I was a true believer. Dressed in a frock coat, black trousers, white shirt, and a black string tie, the requisite wide-brimmed hat balanced on my head. And below my hat, a white rubber mask, pulled tight across my face.

Corrosion

El Hornillo, Texas. With a tattered suitcase in one hand and a Bible in the other, I stood on the top of Black Oil Hill and stared down at the town below, all stuffed full of drunks and whores and rapists and killers. I shook my head and spat on the ground. And then, whispering to the skies, Earth is his, but not forever. I stayed on that hill for some time, just thinking and praying and crying. Then I made my way to town.

* * *

Main Street was putrid, just like I expected, the ground smelling of booze and sex, and for forty days and forty nights, I preached without cessation, and I converted a thousand people at least, pain turning to joy, hell turning to heaven. But there was a devilish woman that I saw from time to time, and she reminded me of someone I used to know, and her heart was hardened. Physical appearance: skin wrinkled and leathery, eyes brown and bloodshot. A healthy helping of rouge, lipstick, and mascara doing nothing to hide the ravaged features of her face. A whore, plain and simple. A whore like the rest of them.

Take off your mask! she said one day. Show me your face! And I stepped off my whiskey carton and walked toward her and said: Ain't nobody would want to see my face. Believe me, lady. A face of pure grotesqueness. This mask is only worn to protect you, understand.

And so I told her a story about a sinner of the worst kind. Drinking, whoring, fighting. A marionette, with the devil as his puppeteer. I said: There was a woman I was involved with. Beautiful young thing. Soul of the purest kind. Trusting as a child. You know, she might have even loved me. But I hadn't found Christ. All I knew were the devil's ways. And I was brutal and cruel. And I did some things to her that are too terrible to mention. Don't you understand? Satan himself was rattling around in my skull! He controlled my every move. Sister, sister, I was well on my way to an eternity of torture, an eternity of wrath!

But then I had a vision! A vision of God himself! And do you know what he told me? Do you know what words he spoke on that frostbitten day? He told me to go to the hardware store, presently, and buy myself a jar of Sterno. And I did what I was told. And he told me to open that jar and spread it directly on my face! This is the truth! Homemade napalm! And then a flick of a match…And this was the word of the Lord! And I followed his word on that day, and I've followed his word every day since! Don't you see? I burned my face, so I wouldn't have to burn my soul!

And this story got the whore good and worked up. She smiled and grabbed her swollen breasts and said, Well, I think you're a goddamn prophet is what you are! I never met anybody like you in my whole life, and that's the truth! Looking for a good time? I can give it to you in spades!

Well, now, I followed her through the streets of El Hornillo, but there was no lust emanating from my loins, only rage from my soul, and we came to this old house of sin, an immense Victorian that might have once been stately, now nothing but a sickly-looking eyesore. And I walked into that filthy house and walked into that filthy room and watched as she downed that flask of filthy bourbon, a pair of golden streaks dribbling down her filthy chin. She dropped the flask on the floor, smiled a spiteful smile, and yanked off her hand-me-down dress. I was filled with nausea, believe me. Okay, Prophet, she said. I ain't got all night. A hundred straight in. Two hundred up the ass.

I scowled and clenched my fists. I don't aim to fornicate with you.

Yeah? Well, what do you aim to do? 'Cause I don't do weird shit.

And so I paced across the grimy room, staring at the woman with contempt from the corner of my eyes. I said: The first thing you've gotta do is stop talking so crudely. A woman of God would never—

A woman of God? That's a real laugh, Prophet!

What you don't understand, I said, my voice barely above a whisper, is that you can't live without Jesus. Not really. I came here…God sent me to…

God sent you here? He sent you to me?

Yes. Yes, that's right. He sent me to save you. He sent me to save all of you.

And the whore snorted. Sure, honey, I'll let you save me. Just as long as the price is right.

It doesn't work that way. You can't whore yourself to God. God is no pimp.

You're right about that, she said, laughing. He's worse than a pimp. A pimp beats you for money. God beats you for adulation.

That there's blasphemy, I said. I don't care if this *is* a whorehouse.

Then she pointed at my face. Why don't you take

248

off that mask, she said. I ain't afraid. I've seen terrible before.

Oh no, I said. Too horrific.

I don't believe you, she said. I think you're a fake.

I'm no fake! I shouted. I'm a prophet of the almighty God! And then I took a step toward her, hands clenched, ready to preach. I slapped the girl hard, driving her to her knees, leaving a welt on her cheek. And I kept right on charging, ready to show her the ways of the Lord, and that's when the whore reached into her purse and came out with a spring-loaded-pearl-handle revolver. She pointed it straight between my eyes. And her hands weren't shaking even a little bit.

Nobody hits me, she said.

A smile spread slowly across my masked face, and I nodded my head. I do apologize, ma'am, I said. But you must understand. The Lord wants to save you. He wants that more than anything in the world. That's why he sacrificed his only son. That's why he sent me.

I don't need no saving, she said. Never did.

Hurriedly she put on her dress, managing to keep the gun pointed at me all the while. You better watch yourself, she said. Prophets don't act that way, they just don't! So I picked up my Bible, threw down a filthy twenty at her feet, and marched right out of that House of Sin. The whore was unconverted, but I guessed it wasn't the last I'd be seeing of her.

*   *   *

Corrosion

That evening was a long one. I sat inside my pick-up truck, dome light on, reading my Bible and jotting down notes for a possible sermon, snorting apricot snuff and swallowing plum brandy. Well, only Jesus was truly sin free...

And then when my eyes were good and tired, and my brain was good and pickled, I closed the Bible and my notebook. I took off my hat and placed it on the seat next to me. Then I removed my rubber mask, placed it inside my hat. Oh Lord, I whispered, how long will you keep me in this purgatory? How long till I prove my worth?

I opened the glove compartment, pulled out an envelope. Inside the envelope a silver chain. Hanging from the chain a dog tag. And on the dog tag, the name of a soldier. Dead now. Buried in an unmarked grave.

I pressed the dog tag to my cheek, felt the coolness of the metal. Then I placed it back in the envelope, sealed it, and returned it to the glove compartment.

I turned off the dome light and leaned back in the seat. Outside, a beautiful moon shone through the mist, and the cold rain fell on the living and the dead.

I closed my eyes and soon I was dreaming of the past, a speck of light in the iron darkness.

ABOUT THE AUTHOR

Jon Bassoff was born in 1974 in New York City. In addition to his work as a writer, Bassoff is also the founder of the crime fiction publisher New Pulp Press. He lives in Colorado with his wife and two children. This is his first novel.

Made in the USA
San Bernardino, CA
29 October 2013